Murder with
TORTURE

"Want to hear about the secret room?" Beth Swanson asked as Diane Montrose got her first glimpse of Ravensnest. "The secret room is cut in the cliff itself. . . .
"No way in or out except through a door at the foot of the stairway, but there are channels cut in the rock to let water flow in or out. The room is below water level at high tide."

"For heaven's sake, Beth—why?"

"They say that earlier Warburtons put the survivors from wrecked ships in there and barred the door. The iron grills have long rusted away, but once they opened and allowed the bodies to be flushed out by the falling tide. . . ."

"Horrible! They'd drown slowly as the tide rose. . . ."

But Beth Swanson's story was only the first terrible secret hidden away in the Mansion of Evil. Behind its stern facade, Ravensnest harbored terrors that were to threaten Diane Montrose's sanity and her life itself. Helpless, she struggled against the evil that came surging out of the Warburton past to claim her beauty for its own.

Mansion
of EVIL

CAROLINE FARR

A SIGNET BOOK from

NEW AMERICAN LIBRARY

TIMES MIRROR

in association with Horwitz Publications

SIGNET TRADEMARK REG. U.S. PAT. OFF. AND FOREIGN COUNTRIES
REGISTERED TRADEMARK—MARCA REGISTRADA
HECHO EN CHICAGO, U.S.A.

Signet, Signet Classics, Signette, Mentor and Plume Books
are published by The New American Library, Inc.,
1301 Avenue of the Americas, New York, New York 10019

First Printing, November, 1966

PRINTED IN THE UNITED STATES OF AMERICA

Mansion
of EVIL

CHAPTER
ONE

"TREGONEY WELCOMES CAREFUL Drivers"; the sign loomed through the bus window as we approached an intersection. Then a road sign appeared, its fingerposts labeled Berlin, Dover, Portsmouth, Paris, Exeter. I wondered what nostalgic immigrant had named these places, just as, perhaps, a homesick Cornishman with nagging memories of his own fishing village, had called this small town Tregoney.

The bus turned off the highway into a neat main street and stopped in front of a hotel. I dragged my single heavy bag from the rack, picked up an overnight bag and my handbag, draped my topcoat over my shoulder and staggered out after the other passengers.

A narrow street opposite the bus stop wound downhill towards the water where I could see the stumpy masts of fishing vessels moored in twin rows at a long wharf. I stared at the houses lining that twisting street. They were small but neat, the roofs of wooden shingles gray with age. They looked as though they could have stood there for two hundred years or more, those houses, with son inheriting from father and following the same ways and the same trade.

Although it was still fall, it was cold in Tregoney. I put down my bags and put on my coat. In my letter of instruction I had been told that the office was directly opposite the bus stop. I went across searching for it, and presently discovered two brass plates beside a stairway that led to the floor above a shoe shop. The first plate belonged to a Dr. Kenneth T. Chester, M. D. I peered at the second in the gloom of a blind passage. Prince, Tregarth & Tregarth, Attorneys at Law, I read.

Looking at it I felt slightly let down. From the ornate letterheads used in our correspondence I had expected better of Mr. Stanley Prince. The stairway was dark, the light above it dim. But the office of Prince, Tregarth & Tregarth improved the impression as I walked in and put down my bags gratefully. The outer office was bright and modern. Through venetian blinds at the windows I could see the small harbor and the sea, and the fishing boats moored at the wharf.

The muted rattle of a typewriter stopped as I came in, and the girl typing smiled at me as she stood up and came from behind her desk.

"Can I help you?" She was blonde and pretty, with merry blue eyes. I was so used to the brown skins of sunny California that her pink and white complexion surprised and pleased me. I returned her smile involuntarily.

"My name is Diane Montrose. I'm from Los Angeles. I was to see Mr. Prince."

"Of course!" she smiled. "Miss Montrose! Mr. Prince is expecting you. I didn't realize it was bus time. We're always so busy here. I hope you had a good trip?" Her eyes roved over me, curious and approving.

"Wonderful."

"Will you come this way, Miss Montrose?"

I left my bags and followed her towards a door at the back of the office. She knocked and looked in.

"Miss Montrose is here, Mr. Prince."

"Miss. . . ?" a deep, pleasant male voice inquired.

"Miss Montrose from Los Angeles, Mr. Prince. She just got in by bus from Portland."

"Of course! The nurse! Come in, Miss Montrose! Beth, could you get us coffee and something to go with it? No doubt Miss Montrose could use something invigorating after her long journey."

"Right away, Mr. Prince."

She held the door open for me, and I went inside. I had expected Mr. Prince to be an old man from his letters. He was in his sixties, I decided. His hair was white but thick, and cut in a crew cut that went with his northern pink and white complexion. His neat business suit looked as though it had just come from the tailor's. Three precise triangles of spotless white handkerchief showed from his top pocket. A briar pipe trailed smoke on an ash tray as he put it down and came around to shake hands with me.

"Welcome to Tregoney, Miss Montrose!" he said heartily. His eyes, a sharp, clear blue, widened momentarily as though in surprise.

Then he brought me a chair and set it near his big desk, an active man given to quick decisive movements. He went back to his own chair and picked up his pipe. When I settled in the chair I found that he was studying me carefully through the blue smoke.

"You don't look like a nurse, Miss Montrose," he said. "At least, you're not what I expected from your letters."

I almost told him that I could say the same about him. He looked more like a successful city executive than a family lawyer in a place like Tregoney, Maine. I had expected grease spots on a rumpled suit, and a small, near-sighted, aging refugee from the Big Time.

I said, smiling: "What did you expect me to look like, Mr. Prince? I hope I haven't disappointed you?"

"Disappointed me? No, not at all, Miss Montrose. You're, uh, younger and . . ." he paused for a moment and hurried on, "more attractive than I expected, but I'm sure that's no disadvantage."

"I did send you copies, but here are my credentials, Mr. Prince."

He made a clucking noise with his tongue and smiled at me. "I'm quite prepared to follow my own judgment," he smiled. But I noticed that he read the diplomas and papers thoroughly just the same. "Let's see, graduated from high school, two years at college, three years at the Medical Center in Los Angeles . . ." He straightened slowly. "Very good. Why did you decide to exchange hospital work for private nursing, Miss Montrose?"

"I want to travel, Mr. Prince. And a nurse can find employment in most places."

"You hope to travel overseas?" For a man with such white hair, his eyebrows as he raised them were surprisingly dark.

"Eventually, yes. But I want to see America first."

"And why the Northeast in particular?"

I shrugged. "Since this is the cradle of Amer-

11

ica, it seemed the best place to start. I've seen most of the West Coast. And the West. I've spent most of my vacations moving about, but I haven't felt like working in any of those places. I'd like to work in New York for a while when my contract ends here. Then in the South. Florida, I think."

"Got it all planned," he said admiringly. "Unless of course, you marry?"

"I don't intend to marry," I said confidently. "At least, not for a few years yet. Nursing doesn't leave much time for . . . well, for social activities."

"Hospital nursing that is," he said smiling. "You might find more time on your hands in private nursing. Especially at Ravensnest. And possibly more opportunity for . . . social activities of the kind you mean."

Cups clattered, and I got up quickly to open the door for the secretary as she came in with a tray.

There were cakes that looked as though they were still hot. The coffee in the percolator smelled fragrant, and there was a small jug of cream. Brown sugar crystals. . . .

"Looks good, eh?" Prince laughed. "I'll bet you're just realizing that it's been a long time since breakfast at Portland? Beth, how are you making out with the Warburton file?"

"Another ten minutes, Mr. Prince."

"Good. I want you to come out to Ravensnest with us to witness the will. By the way, this is my secretary, Beth Swanson."

"Yes, Mr. Prince." She smiled at me and went outside.

"Cream and sugar?"

"Thank you. One spoon please." He handed me a cup. "I'm not taking you from your work here?" I asked anxiously. "I mean, I could take a taxi or a bus to the Warburton home, couldn't I?"

He laughed. "I'm afraid not. Ravensnest is at the end of that particular cliff road. Seven miles from here. No public transport out there. No bus. Not that it matters. I have to go out there this morning on some business. I can introduce you around which you may find helpful. In return I'm going to ask you to witness Mrs. Martha Warburton's signature on an important paper for me. Mrs. Warburton is over seventy years of age, and the nominal head of Ravensnest. The document is her will. It needs, of course, two competent witnesses who are present together when the testator signs. It is safest to call in witnesses who are strangers to the testator, since if either witness was a person likely to benefit under the will he or she would lose that benefit under our property laws. Beth . . . Miss Swanson is coming with us to make the second witness."

"I'd be glad to help, Mr. Prince."

"Good! Then that's settled." He offered me

the dish of cakes. "Your folks don't mind you traveling around by yourself?"

"Well, you see," I began. "Both my parents were in London during the war and were killed in the Blitz. My aunt brought me up, but she died a few years ago, too. So there's really no one to call my folks."

Prince clucked sympathetically. "I'm sorry," he said. "That's too bad. Tell me, did you know the Pearson family in Los Angeles? There was a daughter a bit older than you. She married David Warburton."

I thought for a moment, then shook my head. "No, I don't recall any Pearsons."

"I see. Just wondered." Mr. Prince cleared his throat and changed the subject. "I wanted you to meet Dr. Chester, but he's out and not expected back until late this afternoon. He will see you at Ravensnest tomorrow morning, and tell you about your duties."

"I understand I was to have two patients?"

He nodded. A frown drew his dark brows together momentarily. "I'd like to talk to you about that before we leave, Miss Montrose. Mr. David Warburton is your employer. He is Martha's eldest son, and father of the child Robyn. I want you to understand that clearly before we drive out there. Robyn's mother died two years ago. Linda Warburton, David's wife, was a very beautiful and charming woman. Her death was a great loss to David, and indeed to everyone

14

who knew her. Robyn had been delicate since birth, and her mother's death to a child like Robyn, then six years of age, was a tragedy. You'll realize the psychological effect on Robyn better when you have been at Ravensnest for a while. The house and, between you and me, the Warburton family are not what I'd consider ideal surroundings to rear a sensitive and sickly child. But you'll discover that for yourself soon enough, no doubt. The Warburtons are . . . difficult people."

"The child is an invalid?"

"She's been in bed for some months. But Dr. Chester will explain her case to you. She needs constant nursing. Martha is your other patient, and will be your most difficult one I'm sure."

"What is Mrs. Warburton's trouble?"

"Severe arthritis has crippled her. She can walk only with the help of a stick. Chester says she should be in a wheelchair, but she won't hear of that. She has daily injections, I understand. But again, that's Chester's province, not mine."

"You said that Mr. David Warburton is my new employer, and you hinted that I should remember that. May I ask why, Mr. Prince?"

He coughed, and studied me quizzically. "I just mentioned that the Warburtons are difficult people. It's possible that someone at Ravensnest may resent your presence there. Even Martha was against the idea of a trained nurse.

15

The idea was suggested by Chester and myself to David, who agreed at once. He believes, as we do, that a nurse is needed for his mother as well as for his child—and he's prepared to pay for that, which makes you his responsibility alone. David has a private fortune left him by his mother. That is why I want you to understand clearly that David Warburton is your employer, and that you owe responsibility only to him. The rest of the Warburton family are dependent upon Martha, who alone controls the family assets."

"I must also have a responsibility to Dr. Chester, Mr. Prince."

"Well, yes. Naturally, since Chester is the doctor concerned, there will be the usual doctor-nurse relationship with regard to medical procedures. You will find Chester somewhat different from the doctors you're used to working with in a place like the Los Angeles Medical Center. You may find him a little old-fashioned in comparison. A good man Chester, though! Most of the people around Tregoney were brought into the world by him, and he's become an institution—if at times a rather eccentric one by modern standards."

"Does Mr. David Warburton live at Ravensnest?" I asked.

"Since Linda died, he comes to Ravensnest only at weekends to see his mother and Robyn. You won't see him during the week. The Warburton family is extremely wealthy, and David controls the family properties and investments from an office in New York. Prince, Tregarth & Tregarth handle all the family legal problems throughout the United States. I am their agent here in Tregoney. So if any . . . personal problem arises out there when David is not at Ravensnest—I want you to contact me. If you encounter any unpleasantness, Miss Montrose —remember that I am only as far away as the telephone in your room."

I smiled confidently. "Thank you, Mr. Prince. But a nurse quickly becomes accustomed to working among difficult people, patients or otherwise."

Mr. Prince beamed at me, and stood up. "Fine! I knew I was making the right choice when I suggested a trained nurse and sieved the gold from the dross to find you! Now I think it's time we took you out there to introduce you to Ravensnest."

I followed him back into the outer office, where the blonde girl was repairing her lipstick, a bulging attaché case waiting on the dcsk.

"Everything ready, Beth?" he asked cheerfully.

"Yes, Mr. Prince."

"Got Martha's parcel?"

"Yes, it's in the case."

"Good! I'll bring the car around to the front

of the office. You can look after Miss Montrose, and tell her what a fine old home Ravensnest is."

"I sure will, Mr. Prince." She glanced at me, and winked as he picked up the large case and went out with it.

I smiled at her. "My name is Diane, may I call you Beth?"

Her smile was warm and friendly. "Okay, Diane! And anytime you find that mausoleum on the cliffs driving you up the wall, you must come in to Tregoney and visit."

I laughed. "Of course! But why did you just call Ravensnest a mausoleum? Mr. Prince seems to think it's a fine place."

"I'm afraid Stanley is a little prejudiced. For Prince, Tregarth & Tregarth, Ravensnest is the place from where most, if not all blessings flow," she confided, rolling her eyes comically. "Ravensnest Investments Incorporated are not just our best client. They are 60 percent of our total business, handled through Prince, Tregarth & Tregarth offices in San Francisco, Chicago, New York, Miami, London, and of course Tregoney—where for strategic reasons my boss hovers close to Martha Warburton who sits in the center of the web, like a plump and deadly black widow spider."

"Does that make Ravensnest a mausoleum?" I asked, giggling.

"It made itself one more than two hundred

years ago. You know why they called it Ravensnest? Because of the raven's habit of hiding bright glittery things in its nest. You see, the first Warburtons were wreckers."

I stared at her. "Wreckers?"

"Popular pastime hereabouts, and in Cornwall, England, where the family came from three centuries ago. It was a profitable business once, and the Warburton fortune was founded on it. Of course, if any shipwrecked sailors or passengers got ashore they could not be left around to bear witness. There is an old cemetery on the cliffs not far from Ravensnest that's full of them. Another on Gibbet Island out from Ravensnest Bay. When ships were scarce, they tried a little piracy for relaxation. So there's one Warburton in the Gibbet Island cemetery. It was the gibbet they built to hang him there that gave the island its pleasant name. Since he was the only Warburton dumb enough to get caught and hanged, they left him there in disgust."

I studied her suspiciously as we left the gloom of the stairway for the bright sunshine of the sidewalk. Mr. Prince was just getting out of a late model convertible parked at the curb. He beckoned and smiled.

"But all that was long ago," I said.

"Uhuh! Long, long ago. And the authorities made one mistake. They should have hanged *all* the Warburtons and felled the family tree then and there. Hush now! Let Stanley keep his illusions. . . ."

"Well, you two seem to be getting along well together," Mr. Prince beamed as he took my overnight bag, and the attaché case from Beth Swanson. "Has Beth been telling you about Ravensnest?"

"Yes. It sounds most interesting."

"Oh it is!" he said cheerfully. "A little gloomy in bad weather perhaps—but one of the finest old eighteenth century homes in New England. A well-preserved show place! If ever the Warburtons leave it, I have no doubt the government will preserve it for its historical value. The Warburtons first came to Tregoney from Cornwall. They were sea captains who went into business for themselves ashore here, and did very well too. Perhaps you'd better sit in the back with Beth, Miss Montrose. The drive out to Ravensnest is superb. Beth knows the coast, and can tell you about it as we drive. I can't help you much there. The road is one that takes most of the driver's attention."

"You can say that again!" Beth said as she climbed into the back seat. "Any time I drive out there I have goose pimples for a week."

The road followed the edge of the cliffs once we left the village of Tregoney. Waves crashed among tangled rocks against the cliff face hundreds of feet below us as we drove, or boiled in white frenzy over scattered rocks. Farther out the Gulf of Maine was sprinkled with rocky islands against which the waves pounded in the same fury, even though this morning the sea appeared calm.

The sea here did not have the blue of the Pacific, even this afternoon with the sun shining brightly. The rocks were dark, and glistened from flying spume that we could feel as a fine spray upon our faces.

"The coast of Maine is two hundred and fifty miles long as the crow flies," Mr. Prince said over his shoulder. "But if you could follow the jagged, rocky coastline all the way you'd travel two thousand, four hundred miles. Near enough to ten miles of bays, inlets, headlands and rocky points to every mile."

"And the bones of a lot of ships down there at the foot of the cliffs all the way from New Hampshire to the Canadian border," Beth said. "With most of the wrecks around Ravensnest Bay and Gibbet Island. Ships from Europe, or Canada used to cross the Gulf of Maine westerly from Cape Sable at the southern tip of Nova Scotia on their way to Boston. Navigation was uncertain in those days, and ships often made landfall too far north; to see Cape Cauldron to the north of Ravensnest Bay, and mistake it for Cape Ann just north of Boston. The lights of Ravensnest, and the lanterns of wreckers along the cliffs created the imagined lights of Boston Town. In darkness that was a fatal mistake."

I stared at the tortured coastline and shivered. What had been something of a joke back in the lawyer's office in Tregoney seemed no longer so.

"There's Tern Island," Beth said, pointing. "In the spring the terns nest there and the whole island seems alive and quivering. The island farther out is Captain Quelch's Island. Captain Quelch was a pirate hanged in Boston in 1704. See the point that runs out into the sea ahead? That's Despair Point. They say Nathan Warburton's wife sat there with a telescope to watch him hanged on Gibbet Island. You'll see Gibbet and Ravensnest when we cross Point Despair. Now look farther out to sea and you'll see Cape Cauldron vaguely a long way north. See it?"

"Yes, I see it," I replied, staring. It had looked like low cloud, but took shape slowly as we approached Point Despair as a mass of high cliffs. It was the sea pounding on broken rock at the base of Cape Cauldron that made it hard to see, I realized, obscuring the cliffs by drifting clouds of spray. Cape Cauldron was well named. The whole sea around it seemed boiling in white froth of spurting, breaking waves pounding upon unseen reefs of solid rock.

The car slowed, and I looked ahead again.

"Here's your first sight of Ravensnest, Miss

Montrose," Mr. Prince called cheerfully. "Have you told her about the secret forest, Beth? Or the secret room."

"I was coming to it," Beth Swanson said. "You'll lose sight of Ravensnest again presently. The road turns every which way. Well, what do you think of it?"

"It's huge," I said, awed. "It looks as big as a hospital! There must be a hundred rooms!"

"Forty-seven," Beth said, smiling. "A housekeeper's nightmare, I'd call it. How Mrs. Rathbone looks after it with the staff she has I'll never know."

Ravensnest was huge. Built of red brick, it reared three floors high to the slate roof and the rows of chimneys. Broad stone steps led up to the front doors, sheltered by a porch with an open gallery above supported by white pillars. Other buildings crouched behind it had once been stables, coach houses and the living quarters of the grooms and gardeners. A tower rose like a belfry from the center gable of the roof, overlooking the wide bay beyond sheer cliffs of wet gray stone. . . .

A turn in the cliff road hid Ravensnest abruptly from my sight, and I leaned back again slowly.

"Want to hear about the secret room?" Beth asked. "Did you notice how Ravensnest sits right on the edge of the cliffs? The secret room is cut in the cliff itself. A cell cut from the living rock at the bottom of a stairway shaft. No way in or out except through a door at the foot of the stairway, but there are channels cut in the rock to let water flow in or out. The room is below water level at high tide."

I stared at her. "For Heaven's sake Beth—why?"

"Well, they say that earlier Warburtons put the survivors from wrecked ships in there and barred the door. The iron grills have long rusted away, but once they opened and allowed the bodies to be flushed out by the falling tide to be found later conveniently drowned in the wreck."

"But that would be murder with torture, and horrible! They'd drown slowly as the tide rose. . . ."

"But nobody in Ravensnest would hear them, even if they had not been busy roistering with the ship's cargo, broaching the spirits, feeling the quality of the silks and fine linen, counting the gold. . . ."

"Beth has quite an imagination," Mr. Prince laughed. "Doesn't she? Nothing like that was ever proven against the Warburtons."

"Nathan was convicted of piracy," Beth said patiently, as though it was a matter they argued often. "There was one charge of wrecking in 1689, another in 1752. They failed because the shipowners had no witnesses. Because there were no survivors from the wrecks."

"Piracy was considered respectable once." Mr. Prince said apologetically. "As for the others—it could have been the malevolence of jealous people that started the rumors. After all, we burned witches alive in Tregoney a lot later than that, merely on the information of jealous and ignorant people. Miss Montrose, here is Ravensnest again. Look to your right across Ravensnest Bay, and tell me what you see?"

I stared across at spreading acres of green moving back from the cliffs for miles. Around the nearer edge, dunes of white sand swelled and curved, smoothed by the wind.

I said appreciatively, "They're very beautiful."

Mr. Prince laughed heartily. "That's the secret forest. A beech forest. The wind from the sea is so strong that the young trees bend away from it to grow horizontally instead of vertically. The trunks are full-grown and thick, but very short, and the branches grow into a roof no more than six or eight feet high and all so closely interlocked and twisted together that looking at it even from much closer than this you'd never suspect there were the huge old trunks of the beeches beneath the green surface of your 'Lawn.' "

"Can you walk around in there?" I asked.

"Oh sure," Beth Swanson said quickly. "There's a path in from this side. You could walk for miles in there if you wanted to. Or lose yourself in there. Not that anyone in their right mind would want to do that. It's about the spookiest place I've ever seen. And there's only one known way in or out. All the rest of the way around the forest's edge the bushes and trees snarl and tangle their branches so thickly you would have to cut your way. And the winds and storms have piled sand and mud up so that it's hard to tell whether there is solid mud and sand or the tops of the trees beneath your feet. Not that you could fall through those tangled branches. Nothing could! But it must be as black as the pit under there. It's a crazy place, Diane—best keep away from there. And from the wreckers' paths down the cliffs. The paths are starting to crumble, and the iron pegs the wreckers used to cling to are rusted away."

I laughed. "I'm not going to Ravensnest to explore secret forests or climb cliffs, Beth. I'm going to Ravensnest to *nurse!*"

"That's right," Mr. Prince said. "And here we are, Miss Montrose. Ravensnest. . . ."

The house had appeared again just ahead as the car rounded a bend. A low wall surrounded its cultivated acres, I saw now. We passed through big, green-painted iron gates onto a gravel drive that wound through flower gardens and lawns toward the house standing on a smoothly grassed rise.

I smiled, relieved. Ravensnest looked as neat and normal and well-kept as a hospital. On the

26

upper gallery a group of people sitting around a table started turning their heads towards us as they heard the car. They stared down at us as Mr. Prince parked outside the front steps. Mr. Prince climbed out of the driver's seat and smiled at me as he held my door open.

"Welcome to Ravensnest, Miss Montrose," he said. "I know you'll be happy here, and I hope you decide to stay a long while."

"Thank you," I said, returning Mr. Prince's smile.

There was no reason for the vague uneasiness I felt, like a sense of dread upon me. Maybe Beth Swanson's dislike for the place had distorted my intensified feeling of strangeness at new surroundings. It was like starting work at a new hospital, I told myself firmly.

TWO

MR. DAVID SAID that Miss Montrose was to have a room near Robyn's, Miss Swanson," the maid said, smiling at Beth Swanson.

"I thought Mrs. Rathbone would have met Miss Montrose, Molly," Beth said, frowning slightly. "Where is Mrs. Rathbone? She's not out is she?"

"Why no, miss," the maid said uneasily. She was blonde and petty, and the black, old fashioned maid's uniform with its frilly cap, and the frills of white at her wrists made her look like smart ladies' maids of more formal days I had seen on television or the films. "Mrs. Rathbone is planning dinner right now. She said she'd see Miss Montrose later." She glanced at me obliquely, but her gray blue eyes were friendly enough. "Mrs. Rathbone said Miss Montrose wouldn't be expected to take over her duties until Dr. Chester calls tomorrow."

"I'd like to meet my patients today, if that's possible," I said. "Do you think it is, Molly?"

"Of course, Miss Montrose. But aren't you to see Mrs. Warburton with Mr. Prince this afternoon?"

Beth nodded. "That's right, Molly. In ten minutes. Mr. Prince is with her now. We're to go down when Miss Montrose's things are in."

"Fine," Molly smiled doubtfully. "Well, I'll show you Robyn's room on the way, Miss Montrose. And then Mrs. Rathbone says you will join Mr. Prince on the gallery for coffee."

Beth's frown faded slowly. "Well, okay! Rathbone seems to have arranged everything." She said it with most of her doubt gone.

The maid smiled again. "This way, please. . . ."

The stairs we climbed from the entrance were wide and thickly carpeted. The balustrade of the stairway was of marble, and a painting with the richly dark colors of an old master hung on the wall where the stair turned towards an upper gallery. Beneath the painting an urn stood on a marble pedestal, and a riot of pink and dark red blooms trailed from the pelargonium it contained.

We turned into a passage with doors opening

on either side. The sound of the sea grew stronger as we walked. But the carpet seemed to deaden its roar as it muffled our footsteps.

"This is Miss Robyn's room, Miss Montrose," the maid whispered as we neared the end of the passage. She pointed ahead to the last door on our left. "Mr. David has the room next to hers. It's part of a large suite really. Mr. David lived in there with his wife and Robyn, and he still uses it when he comes to Ravensnest. Your room is directly opposite, across the passage. You'll find it's quite nice. It has one of the best views from Ravensnest, since it looks out to sea. Mr. David chose the opposite view when he married." She glanced at Beth as though they shared some secret. "Mr. David hates the sea."

"Could I see Robyn now?" I asked as she unlocked the door of my room.

"Robyn is asleep, Miss Montrose. She always sleeps in the afternoon for a couple of hours. Dr. Chester's orders."

She opened the door and as we followed her inside I stared around curiously. The room was huge, with great windows at which heavy lace curtains moved sluggishly in a breeze from the sea. Heavy wainscoting in panels of rich dark red covered the walls to the picture rail. Two pictures of the Louis XIV period portrayed a scene at some masked ball at the French Court, the black masks giving the figures a peculiarly sinister impression of shallowness and the pursuit of pleasure.

The furniture was of the same period, all spindly legs and curves, with accent upon a magnificent mirror at the dressing table.

"Bryant is bringing up your bags, Miss Montrose," she said cheerfully. "I aired the room this morning. The rooms are so close to the sea on this side of the house that Mrs. Rathbone told me to use lavender. She thought the room smelled musty. You have your own bathroom through here. Clean towels are in here. . . ."

She moved about busily, but it was Beth who followed her, not me. I stayed at the window, staring out. The view was breathtaking. A small, stone-walled courtyard lay below my window, and between the parted green shutters I could see the clifftop only a few yards beyond. As I watched I heard a faint hissing sound, and a white column rose from the cliff and fell back again. Startled, I stared down and presently the phenomenon was repeated. White water was being thrown up in a waterspout at regular intervals in time with the big waves rolling in below the cliffs.

Beth noticed me staring down, and presently joined me curiously. "What's doing that?" I asked.

She looked away. "There's a . . . a sort of cavern down there, Diane. Water is driven into it by the waves, and at high tide as it is now the pressure forces the air and water already in the cave up through a . . . well, a sort of chimney. They call it the blowhole."

I looked at her suspiciously: "It wouldn't be . . . the *cell* you mentioned earlier?"

"Well, yes," she said slowly. "It is. I didn't want to frighten you." She shuddered. "Ugh! What a view! This whole place does something to me. I've only been out here three or four times, but I can't get away quick enough. Why don't you ask old Rathbone to give you another room?"

I glanced out into the passage through the open door, and shook my head. "I was just curious, that's all. I don't want to change. This room is convenient to my patients. Or to one of them at least." I looked at the maid. "Where does Mrs. Martha Warburton have her room, Molly?"

"First door on the left as you come into this passage, Miss Montrose. Only like Mr. David's, it's a suite of rooms. Mrs. Warburton spends most of her time there. Bryant and I helped her downstairs to the study earlier, but it's the first time she's been downstairs this week, the poor lady!"

"Which hasn't sweetened her disposition any, I suppose?" Beth asked, smiling at the look on the girl's face.

She flushed, and forced a smile. "She wasn't very well this morning. The pain makes her

... difficult." She glanced at me quickly. "Here comes Bryant with your bags, Miss."

He was a rather good-looking young man in his middle-twenties wearing what looked like a hospital orderly's white uniform coat over dark trousers.

Beth said; "Hello Ken."

"Hello Miss Swanson," he replied cheerfully. He was freckled and sandy-haired, with a snub nose and a wide, contagious grin. "Mrs. Rathbone said Mrs. Warburton Senior wants Miss Montrose and you in the study." He glanced at me sympathetically. "I wouldn't be too long about getting there, if I were you. I have seen Mrs. Warburton happier."

"First, meet Miss Montrose, Ken," Beth said. "She's a friend of mine, and I want you to look after her for me. Diane, this is Ken Bryant. His folks live next-door to mine in Tregoney."

I said: "Hello Ken." We shook hands, with Molly Waters watching doubtfully. There might be a romance there, I smiled to myself as I left for the study with Beth.

Despite Beth Swanson's gloomy excerpts from the Warburton-Ravensnest past, I told myself firmly that the place seemed well-kept and normal, the people like those you meet anywhere else. It was a long time since the Warburton family had been wreckers and pirates, or since Ravensnest had witnessed violence and murder. Or since that infernal chimney at the base of the cliff had thrown a body into the sea. . . .

Out in the passage I hesitated, then stopped at Robyn's door.

"Diane, do you think you should?" Beth asked with an edge of anxiety.

"I don't see why not."

"Well, Martha isn't the kind of woman you keep waiting."

I opened the door. The room was furnished as a nursery still, with fairyland and bunny-rabbit murals on the walls, and cuddly toys in a glassed cabinet. It would have been better suited to a four-year-old than the child in the bed against the wall. She was sleeping deeply, one thin arm above the covers and a mass of blonde hair framing her placid face against the pillow. Her skin had that almost transparent look that chronically sick children often acquire.

Pity touched me unexpectedly, although I did not know why. I had seen many children who were obviously sicker. But there was an innocence, a sad quality in that sleeping face that touched me deeply. I closed the door again slowly.

"You didn't frighten her?" Beth asked in an anxious whisper.

"She's asleep," I said quietly.

Beth Swanson looked at me curiously for a moment, then nodded silently. We walked on.

I must beware of pity for this child, I thought. In hospitals I had been too busy to harbor pity in my mind, except briefly and on rare occasions. Pity can be dangerous. Sympathy, a wish to share the patient's burden can destroy you as a nurse.

"She's lovely, isn't she?" Beth Swanson said in a low voice. "Spoiled a little, maybe. But she's naturally such a sweet, innocent kid that you don't seem to notice."

"They seem to be treating her as a child of four, instead of a girl of eight," I said. "That isn't good."

She smiled at me. "That's David. He's really a dear, Diane. He's the only Warburton I know well—the rest of them don't have much to do with us in Tregoney." She paused thoughtfully. "Sometimes I think David wants to keep her a baby. His world now begins and ends with Robyn. I'd hate to think what he'd do if anything happened to her. That's why Stanley and Dr. Chester arranged for you to come here. David has always been the rebel of the Warburton family, and he was terribly in love with Linda before Robyn came along. After Robyn was born, I think he worshipped her. Did you know that Robyn was with David when they found Linda's body?"

I stared at her. "What do you mean—found her body?"

"Shh!" she murmured. "The library is just

ahead! I thought you knew that Linda drowned. Apparently she used to go down the cliff path over near the secret forest to a small beach. On sunny days she'd sunbathe down there if the weather was warm enough. The day she died, David and Robyn went down to share the walk back with her. But there'd been an accident. Linda had fallen before she reached the path down. David found her in shallow water at the edge of the beach. It was Robyn who saw her first."

"Good God!"

"Mr. Prince should have told you that," Beth said in the same low voice. "I suppose he didn't want to spoil your first day at Ravensnest. He's probably left it to Dr. Chester to tell you."

We had reached a closed door to the right of the stairway. She stopped and looked at me anxiously.

"I won't say anything," I promised, frowning.

"Good."

She knocked, and Mr. Prince's hearty voice answered. I followed her inside slowly, and glanced around. A fire blazed in a great open fireplace, and the chairs were deep and upholstered in leather. A huge table of Chinese blackwood as dense as stone stood in the middle of the room. The legs supporting it were rampant dragons; with the light of the fire flickering on them they seemed alive. But it was the books that took my attention in that first glance. Except for the window space that looked out upon the green lawns and rose gardens, shelves of leather-bound books covered the walls to a height of eight feet or so. I felt as though I had stepped straight into the eighteenth century. I stared at the books fascinated.

"You were a long time coming," a woman's harsh voice said testily. "And are you a nurse, or a librarian?"

She was a tall woman, with snow-white hair, and fierce brown eyes that were studying me with angry insolence. She sat bolt upright on the edge of one of the big leather chairs at the head of the great table staring at me. She wore black— a long-sleeved dress from the sleeves of which protruded the bent claws of arthritic hands. A gold wedding ring, and a white cameo brooch on a plain gold chain about her scrawny neck were her only ornaments.

"I'm a trained nurse, Mrs. Warburton," I said. "Mr. Prince has seen my credentials. It's just that the books surprised me. I've never seen a library like this before."

"One of the most valuable private collections in the country, Miss Montrose," Mr. Prince said, pushing back his chair and standing up. "Mrs. Warburton, this is Miss Montrose, the nurse Mr. David has employed to look after Robyn and—uh, see that you have your injections regularly. . . ."

"The more fool David," she snorted. "A nurse is not needed here. I've looked after Robyn for eight years. Something her fool mother could never do efficiently while she was alive! And as for nursing *me*, girl—just you try it!" She looked at me briefly with her dark eyes snapping. "Well, if these are your witnesses, Stanley, let's get started!"

Beth said sweetly as we sat down on the two empty chairs: "Good morning Mrs. Warburton."

"Hello! Are you still at the Tregoney office? Thought you would have married by now. At your age I had a man of my own, and had started on my second pregnancy. Your own grandmother was married at seventeen as I recall it; I declare, each generation becomes weaker and more useless. Why haven't you married, Elizabeth Swanson? No young men in Tregoney these days?"

Beth flushed to her hairline. "These days we wait for the men to ask," she said deliberately.

Mrs. Warburton gave her a long, speculative look. "Don't wait too long, Elizabeth."

The flush on Beth's face deepened, and I waited sympathetically for the explosion. But Mr. Prince cleared his throat noisily, and rustled the papers before him.

"Well, well, as Mrs. Warburton has said,

shall we get on with the business in hand, ladies?" Mr. Prince's face had acquired a pink tinge.

My eyes met Mrs. Warburton's unexpectedly across the table, and momentarily I thought I saw an amused mischievous malice there before I looked away.

"Oh then get on with it, Stanley," she said. "And stop wasting our time."

"Yes," Prince said uneasily. "Well, this document before me is the last will and testament of Martha Therese Warburton, widow, of Ravensnest in the County of Tregoney, Maine, revoking all previous wills as at the time of signature. You Elizabeth Swanson, and you Diane Montrose have been called to witness Martha Therese Warburton's signature on this her last will and testament. The law provides that the testator's signature must be made in the presence of two witnesses present together at the time of signing as you are now, and that you both understand clearly this is Martha Therese Warburton's last will, revoking all others. Is that understood?"

"Yes," I said.

Beth muttered: "Yes!" Her anger was fading slowly.

"You must both sign the will as witnesses in the presence of the testator, as she must sign in your presence. And since this is a long will, each page must be signed and witnessed separately at its foot. Now if you're ready, Mrs. Warburton?"

It was painful to watch those cramped and swollen fingers grip the pen. She wrote slowly, and without the use of glasses frowning in concentration, or perhaps from pain.

"Beth, you sign here as witness."

Beth signed.

"Miss Montrose, please."

I took the document and the pen. Beth's signature was a quick scrawl, but Martha Warburton's I saw with surprise was copperplate, precise and beautiful. I signed, hesitated over the address. . . .

"Occupation Registered Nurse," Mr. Prince prompted me quietly. "Address Ravensnest, Tregoney, Maine, U.S.A. . . ."

"Temporarily," Martha Warburton said. "If Kerr, or Daphne or any of them try to contest it, you'll be short one witness, you'll never find her, Stanley. All nurses are fly-by-nights."

"I have no doubt that Miss Montrose can be found if ever that should occur," Mr. Prince said stiffly. "The Nurses' Association would trace her for us. Now this page. Sign again. . . ."

"I've known nurses who spent the whole of their useful life in the same hospital, Mrs. Warburton," I said quietly as I signed.

"So you're a hospital nurse, eh?"

"Yes, Mrs. Warburton."

"Where at?" She was staring at me curiously, I thought.

"Los Angeles Medical Center. California."

"Miss Montrose has the very best credentials, Mrs. Warburton," Mr. Prince said. "None better that we could find. Now this page please. . . ."

"Let her talk for herself, Stanley. She's going to need to do that after you're gone. And no doubt she can. She's got the dour look, almost like a true Warburton. Any Welsh blood in your veins, girl? Or Cornish?"

"American mostly," I said, flushing.

"Rubbish! All good American stock started someplace else, and the best of it came from England."

"A lot of good Americans don't think so," I said.

"No? Well, that's what we think at Ravensnest. Montrose? Where did the name originate?"

"Scotland, I've been told. The Montrose family were Highlanders and for Charles against Cromwell. Those who survived came here."

"You see?" she said with a grim satisfaction, as though she'd wrung it from me. I stared at her angrily.

"Scotland isn't Cornwell, or Wales!"

She wrote the final signature, ignoring me, and Beth and I witnessed it. Mr. Prince straightened, satisfied, and started gathering his papers.

41

"Thank you Miss Montrose, Beth; Mrs. Warburton, I'll deposit these documents with the bank this afternoon as usual."

"You bring anything else with you, Stanley?"

"Yes." He brought out the parcel that had bulged his briefcase, and I saw that it was an oblong box carefully wrapped.

She glanced at it and nodded. "Put it in the safe for me like a good fellow, Stanley."

The safe was a round one in the wall behind a picture where the shelves ended over near the windows. I discovered her examining me as he opened it, and looked away, embarrassed. But it had been the parcel that interested me. Liquid sounds had come from it.

"The other members of my family are upstairs on the gallery," she said. "They're discussing what we're doing down here of course.

"No doubt they're sweating up there! Did you type this document, Elizabeth? They don't know the will's contents—and I don't mean them to." She smiled maliciously at Beth and me.

Beth flushed. "I typed the schedules, Mrs. Warburton. Not the will. But if you think I would. . . ."

Mr. Prince said quickly: "I typed the will, Mrs. Warburton. But only because that was your instruction. I trust Miss Swanson implicitly."

She ignored that. But she glanced at him.

"Good. So far you've always managed to be discreet, Stanley. And you'd better continue to be, if you want to keep on handling my affairs for me."

"You can rely on my discretion," Mr. Prince said, his pink and white complexion deepening.

"How about you, Miss Montrose?" The sharp brown eyes looked into mine abruptly. "You take a peek when you were signing? I noticed that Stanley covered each sheet, but it seems to me you have sharp eyes. Eyes trained to obeserve."

I went as red as Beth abruptly, and with the same quick anger. Martha Warburton seemed to possess the ability to make people furious with a single word or glance, and she delighted in doing just that.

"My only interest was in witnessing your signature," I told her coldly. "I did that only because Mr. Prince was kind enough to drive me here. I did not look higher than the signatures. But I have not the slightest interest in the contents of your will. If I'm going to nurse here, knowledge like that would only be an embarrassment. I'm not a fool, Mrs. Warburton."

"Hmm!" she said, with the brown eyes needling me. "That's true! You're no fool. Very well, we'll leave it at that. What you haven't seen can't get you into any trouble at Ravensnest, can it? But some of my dear relatives are going to be awfully curious. They'll ask you

43

plenty of questions about it if they get the chance. And they're not going to believe what you tell 'em either. You'll find them persistent. This happens to be the first will I've made since Robyn, my only grandchild, was born. Well, as I said—let them sweat. What people like that need is someone to hold a stick over their heads every now and then. A threat like that is good for their souls. We will join them up on the gallery now." It was obviously an order, not an invitation.

I moved to help her instinctively as she struggled to her feet, but she glared at me savagely.

"I don't need help, Miss Montrose! Remember that please."

She was groping for something beside her; it was a stout walking stick of some dark and ancient wood, carved in a pattern of serpents. Her tightened lips expressed the pain I knew she must be feeling. Prince made an involuntary movement to help her, but stopped the movement so quickly that I realized her stubborn independence was something he knew and understood.

She walked leaning heavily upon the stick, but with her painful movements seeming as firm and determined as though pain did not exist. But I knew better than that as I walked behind her with Beth. She climbed the stairs slowly, her right hand gripping the marble rail, the stick in her left hand helping her climb. It left deep impressions in the carpet.

But when we reached the floor above, she rested briefly and straightened slowly to her full height. She was taller than I had thought, and must have been both a regal and a beautiful woman once. She might have a hateful habit of annoying people, but I could not help admiring her courage as, gesturing to me to remain by the door, we went out onto the gallery, and the eyes of the people there turned quickly to study her calm face.

There were four people at the table, two men, who stood quickly as Mrs. Warburton came out, and two women. The older man might have been sixty. He had dark hair, turned white at the temples, with a single thick lock of white hair that drooped left above eyes that for their sharp and malevolent brown matched Martha's. His face had the same deep lines as Martha's, and the mouth the same slightly sneering twist. He was tall, more than six feet tall, but without Martha's extreme thinness.

The other man was younger, his face weaker, though his mouth had that slightly sarcastic twist that seemed perpetual with Martha Warburton. His hair was blue-black, and shone in the sunlight. Unlike the older man and Martha Warburton he was starting to grow soft and heavy, though he could not yet be forty.

45

The women were both attractive blondes; the younger, about twenty-five, had the kind of large and slightly protruding blue eyes that I have always disliked in a blonde.

The other woman was older, thirty or thirty-five, an assured woman with the brown eyes of a Warburton, and blonde hair that looked darker at the roots where it parted. She was well-groomed, obviously sophisticated, and her legs and figure were those of a show girl.

The younger man laughed and came around the table to move Martha Warburton's chair respectfully. I expected her to refuse, but she allowed him to place it and move her gently as she sat down, accepting his help as though it was a time-honored right.

"You look tired, Martha," he said. "Prince, what have you been doing to her down there? The stairs are too much for her."

There was no affection in his tone. It sounded more like an opening gambit.

"Rubbish," Martha Warburton snorted. "When I can't move around Ravensnest any more the time will have come to bury me! And you know it."

"May that day be many years ahead, Martha," he said glibly. "But you did look tired when you came in. In fact you looked quite ill. Your business with Prince must've been quite a chore. You should let me take more of the administration of this place off your hands, you know. I'm always telling you that."

"Administration like the writing of a new will? Much as you might like to do that for me, Kerr, you know as well as I do that's impossible."

"It's not often I agree with Kerr," the older man said abruptly. "But he's right, Martha. You should allow one of us to take over the administration of Ravensnest. And as your husband's brother, I. . . ."

His voice could have been Martha's, made deeper and more masculine.

"Perhaps you will, when I'm gone, Clive," she interrupted. She glanced up in time to catch the vicious glare that Kerr gave the older man, and smiled. "And perhaps also, it's time that Kerr took over part of the administration of the family investments." She watched Kerr's jealous glance become abruptly triumphant before she shook her head. "Perhaps," she said. "But then again, until I am gone things will remain exactly as they have been."

Kerr stopped abruptly on his way back to his own chair. "I suppose that means you're not going to tell us what's in the new will?"

Martha laughed without mirth. "My dear son, that is exactly what I mean. A will speaks from death. And that is what I intend mine to do. Not before. Where is Rathbone with our coffee? Oh yes, and I have a surprise for you."

She beckoned to me, and I stepped out of the doorway and started towards them.

There was silence as they turned to face me. It was broken by the sharp clatter of a chair falling over and the older man was on his feet. His face was drained of color and his eyes were startled. I stopped uncertainly a few feet from the table.

"God!" he exclaimed in a harsh whisper. "You . . . I can't. . . ." He straightened up, passing a hand across his eyes, visibly trying to regain his control. "I do beg your pardon," he gave a short nervous laugh and glared briefly at Mrs. Warburton. "For a moment there you reminded me very much of someone I, uh, we used to know."

Puzzled, I looked at the other faces—the three strangers startled, Mr. Prince embarrassed, Beth perplexed and Mrs. Warburton . . . Martha Warburton was watching her four relatives as a cat watches a cornered mouse. A humorless smile twisted her mouth and her eyes were hard.

"This is Miss Montrose," she said softly, "the nurse David has employed to look after Robyn. Miss Montrose, this is Kerr, my younger son. All he ever does that's useful is hold my chair for me. He should be quite good at it," her tone was biting, "since he's been doing it for most of his life. And this is my brother-in-law, Clive. Kerr's wife Daphne. Clive's daughter, Isabel. . . ."

I smiled uncertainly to the murmured chorus of "how do you do?" Clive Warburton bowed stiffly and Kerr came around to shake my hand.

"You're far, far too attractive for a children's nurse, Miss Montrose." His low voice was as smooth and oily as his slicked-back, perfumed hair. I shrank from contact with him, but could not avoid his outstretched hand. As he led me to a chair, I caught his wife's gaze. She had obviously overheard her husband's remark and her china-blue eyes were resentful.

The tension I sensed around me was eased by the appearance of Molly with a wheeled tray. It was loaded with fragile cups, a pot of steaming coffee and dishes of fresh, buttered biscuits and cakes.

Behind Molly and her quick, warm smile I saw Mrs. Rathbone for the first time. She wore a plain black dress tight at the throat and wrists. She was as thin and tall as Martha. A pale-skinned woman, her hair was as black as Martha's was white, but with the dead, luster-less black of dyed hair. Her eyes were an almost amber brown like the eyes of a hawk I'd seen once, eyes that seemed incapable of expression. Cruel eyes, I decided, that went with the tight mouth, the hooked nose, the downward lines from the mouth's corners that portrayed sul-

lenness and a contained anger. The only orna-
ment she wore was a white cameo brooch on
thin gold chain.

"Miss Montrose," Martha's dry voice said.
"This is Mrs. Rathbone, my housekeeper."

Uncertainly I said: "How do you do, Mrs.
Rathbone." I felt unsure of my position here,
of whether I was sitting at this table as guest or
servant. Mrs. Rathbone inclined her head
slightly.

"Miss Montrose's room is ready, Mrs. Warburton. Bryant carried up her bags. Molly has
shown her to her room." So far as Mrs. Rathbone was concerned, I might not have been
there.

The conversation became slowly more general. Isabel Warburton asked me a question
about nursing, and her father asked where I
had nursed. When I told them Los Angeles,
Kerr and his wife became interested, and ques-
tioned me briefly about Los Angeles and Hollywood, which neither had seen. Only Clive
was silent, making little further effort to join
in the small talk.

I was glad when Martha Warburton groped
for her stick and stood up. The others were
already talking together in low voices as we left
the gallery. I said good-bye to Mr. Prince and
Beth out at the car.

Beth said in a low voice as Mr. Prince
climbed into the driver's seat: "They sure

haven't improved any since the last time I was out here, Diane! I hope you have a clause in your contract that allows you to leave with your salary. I'll give you a month at Ravensnest. Two at most. Promise you'll come and visit when it gets too tough?"

"I promise," I said gratefully. I felt as though I was losing my only friend. "Beth, what was all that business about on the gallery?"

"I don't know, I was hoping you'd be able to tell me! Clive looked as though he'd seen a ghost."

"Well, you'll soon settle in here," Mr. Prince said loudly and enthusiastically. "Actually, your duties don't start until David gets here. You'll find it will be different then, a lot different. David is a likable guy, and knows exactly what he's doing. He's not like the others. In the meantime, I suggest you look around Ravensnest and get to know your way about. None of the others will interfere in any way. Just do what you please. Take a walk along the cliff path. You'll find the view worthwhile. And don't forget what I told you! Any problems, any time—you call me in Tregoney! Right?"

"Right," I said. "Thank you, Mr. Prince. Good-bye. Good-bye, Beth. . . ."

I watched the car go and walked slowly up the stairs. I glanced into the child's room and

51

found her still sleeping. I closed my own door behind me gratefully. Outside my window a hissing noise startled me, and I went to the window and glanced out anxiously. The thin white column of water leapt high into the air, remaining suspended at its zenith for a second before it fell deliberately back into the sea.

I started to unpack slowly, reluctantly. . . .

behind me gratefully. Outside my windo

CHAPTER

THREE

AMONG THE ROCKS below me as I walked I could see the white of broken water whirling, being sucked far out again in streaming froth. In the deeper and more sheltered pools broad leaves of kelp waved slowly far down like beckoning, yellow-green arms. The path was broad and seemed well used, and for the first few hundred yards from the gates of Ravensnest a low stone wall guarded the edge and the drop to the water and the waiting fangs of rock far below.

Out across Ravensnest Bay I could see Gibbet Island thrusting up out of the sea with the broken water of reefs stretching away from its northern side towards Cape Cauldron's haze of flying spume. The island looked like some great crouching animal. Its northern end rose to a height of two hundred feet or more, a wooded slope that ended in sheer cliffs falling to the sea. But on the south and the southeast the island sloped back to the water gently, grassed, and with a small beach facing me, seeming to afford a fair enough anchorage sheltered from the prevailing winds by the island's bulk.

It would be to that beach, I decided, that once wreckers had gone out to pick over the bones of ships dying on the reefs or against the rock walls at the northern end. And it would have been there also that the redcoats had taken Nathan Warburton for hanging long ago, for above the beach across a grassy slope I could see symmetrical shapes of what must be headstones. I found myself looking for the gibbet instinctively, and shivered. But that was foolish. Its timbers would have rotten to dust years before. Nothing remained on Gibbet Island now save the bones of the dead, and the headstones that marked where they lay, known or unknown.

I remembered suddenly that David Warburton's wife had died here, somewhere where I walked. Her body had been found on a small beach where she came to sunbathe when she could, glad I supposed to escape from the house behind me, as I had been glad when I left it to walk along the cliff path.

I walked faster, remembering what Beth had told me. My mind starting to picture the agony of the child and the husband when they found her. It could not have happened here, the path was too broad, too safe, even though in parts it was damp underfoot from the sea. Even when I walked away from the path and close to the edge to look down it still seemed safe to me.

Ahead the path narrowed slightly. It moved closer to the edge, and I realized that I was close to the secret forest that Beth had mentioned. I could see its green edge a hundred yards or so away to the left and ahead of me. I turned that way, staring at it. It still looked like grass, but grass of an unusual dark green with wide leaves I saw as I came closer. . . .

I felt the ground sink beneath me abruptly. I cried out and drew back with my heart pounding in a sudden fear. It felt as though I were walking on a spring mattress. I drew back carefully, testing with my weight, finding a definite edge to that springy crust. I stood on firm ground again, staring at where I had walked. I had left only very slight footprints there, though I was sure I had sunk at least a foot.

I had not given Beth's secret forest much thought at the time, but I did now. For that grass I was staring at *was* the thickly tangled and interlaced branches of beech trees. And for beeches to grow such a web of branches, such a thick carpet of green leaves there had to be huge trunks there someplace beneath what appeared to me to be ground level.

There were beeches in the garden at Ravensnest, massive old trees with huge trunks that must have been at least two centuries old. The trunks had great girth, but their foliage and branches spread wider than any beech tree I had ever seen, so that they seemed distorted into great umbrellas with little height. The effect of the driving wind from the sea must have been even more pronounced here on the open cliff-top.

I shuddered, backing away from the mattress of tangled treetops, and walked on down the path.

This, I decided, was indeed a crazy place! One day though, I would find a way into the secret forest and see what it was like in there. Someone at Ravensnest would know the way inside.

But I saw a crescent of clean white sand below me suddenly and forgot the secret forest. Slips led up from the sea to a boathouse, and there were a couple of skiffs pulled far back away from the lunging sea.

It must have been from this beach that the wreckers had put to sea long ago. The ribs of several small boats lay like gaunt skeletons behind the beach. The newer skiffs must be used for fishing by the present generation, for lobster pots lay near the skiffs, and a mesh net hung to dry on poles behind the boat-shed. And as I looked down a man came from the boat-shed carrying a box; he set it down to sit on and started repairing the drying net. He puffed on a pipe as he worked, with the blue smoke drifting up, making a picture of contentment and peace against the background of gray rock, white sand and gently heaving green sea.

I smiled, feeling relief unexpectedly. I started looking for the way down, and presently found steps hewn in the rock with an iron handrail on one side winding down to the sand below.

Perhaps it was here that Linda Warburton had fallen to her death. It was steep enough, with a drop of perhaps two hundred feet, and there were rocks below. But I frowned as I descended the steps, puzzled. Anyone unfortunate enough to fall here would have certainly been killed—but on the rocks, not by drowning. The debris that marked the waterline of high tide and big seas lay far beyond where any body that might have fallen from here could have reached. If Linda Warburton had fallen here, her body would not have been found in the sea.

I decided that she must have fallen back along the path. Perhaps some trick of the tide had sucked her out, and carried her body to the beach to rest. But I found myself gripping the rail nevertheless, with my knuckles white, and my breath coming fast, although normally I have no fear of heights. And I breathed deeply in relief when at last I stepped down on soft, dry sand.

I walked slowly towards the fisherman and his net. He was using a wooden instrument to repair the net, his fingers working nimbly as he looped and tied with his head bent, intent on the task. He was muttering to himself as he worked, like a man accustomed to being alone by the sea. I stopped a few yards away.

"Excuse me. . . ." He worked on, absorbed, and I raised my voice. "Hello there!"

He turned, startled. I watched his ruddy face change swiftly. His eyes widened, his tanned face changed abruptly to a sickly, yellowish gray. He cried out, dropped the net and momentarily I thought he was about to fall from his box. I moved involuntarily to help him, but he drew away from me, shaking.

"Are you all right? I'm sorry I frightened you! Lean forward. Bend your head as low as you can. Please? I'm a nurse. . . ."

"An . . . nurse? I thought she. . . !"

He allowed me to bend his head and shoulders forward. He started to relax slowly.

"Is that better?"

"Yes, miss . . . okay now," he mumbled sickly.

"Keep your head down for a minute. You could feel faint again if you straighten too quickly," I urged as he tried to sit up.

"I'm . . . okay! But you sure scared me, looking the way you do, and me thinking of *her* just then, and. . . ."

I let him straighten slowly. His color was still bad, and sweat beaded on his forehead. He raised one arm heavily, and wiped the sweat away with his sleeve.

"Is there water in the boathouse? Can I get you a drink?"

He shook his head. "Who are you, miss? Someone from Ravensnest?"

"Robyn's nurse. Have you had attacks like this before?"

"No, miss. Nothin' the matter with me. It was just seeing you that way of a sudden, and. . . ."

"And thinking I was . . . someone else?"

He was silent.

"Please tell me," I begged, and in spite of myself my voice started to shake. "Ever since I arrived people have been staring at me like that—as though they'd seen a ghost."

"I thought you were Mr. David's wife," he muttered. "That's what I thought." He glanced at me. "But you're new here. You wouldn't know about that. She used to come here a lot. There was an accident. . . ."

"I heard about it. She fell from the cliff, didn't she? She was drowned?"

"That's what they said."

"You weren't here that day, then?"

"In a manner of speaking, yes and no," he said. His color was coming back slowly. He stared at me. "I was out at Gibbet taking up lobster pots. They'd found her here dead when I got back. Mr. David and Robyn. He was like a crazy man, he was. And Robyn sobbing her little heart out on the beach. It was a terrible thing."

I nodded. "I can imagine, I was thinking of it as I walked down here." I hesitated. "Are you here often, Mr.——?"

"Bob Jensen, miss." He glanced towards the boathouse. "I live there. Look after the boats like my father and my grandfather before me. Yeah, reckon I'm here most of the time. 'Cept when I drive down to Tregoney. I don't eat at the house. I like it better here where I belong."

I held out my hand. "I'm Diane Montrose, Bob."

He took my hand gingerly. His fingers could have been carved from wood, and my hand felt their calluses, even though his hand was gentle. I looked at him curiously. He was a big man, in his fifties, still lean and strong from his work—a sandy-haired man with the thick hair fading back from his forehead, and the look of distance and the sea in deep-set blue eyes above a tanned and pleasant face.

"Here to look after Robyn, are you?"

"Yes, and Mrs. Warburton."

"You're what they both need, I reckon," he smiled uncertainly. "Though maybe the old lady won't think so. Her being hard to get along with the way she is, and full of suspicion and hate for everyone except Robyn and Mr. David. Yet there's another side to old Martha. I've seen it and I know. When my wife died she was good to me. So maybe you'll be the exception and get along with her."

"I hope so, Bob," I said, smiling at him. "I suppose you saw a lot of David's wife."

"That I did, miss. She came here most every chance she got. And glad to get away from the family, I'd say. *And* Mr. Kerr. Sometimes we'd talk. A fine young woman Linda Warburton was, no matter what they say. None better. And lovely to look at. She had hair that shone like a raven's wing, sort of blue-black. And big gray eyes. She wore her hair short and sort of free like yours too. That's why you gave me such a scare. I was thinking about her, and what a goddamn shame it all was. And thinking how I never could find out how she got down here in the sea that day without me seeing her walking along the cliff path, and me expecting her. I was looking for her, you see. And I still got good enough eyes to see anyone on the cliff path from the Gibbet reefs."

I frowned. "You were expecting her that day, Bob?"

He nodded. "We had a storm here the day before, miss. One of those quick summer storms that come out of the sea beyond the islands. She was down here sunbathing, and she got caught. So I loaned her my slicker to wear back to Ravensnest, and she said she'd bring it back the next day for sure. Only they found her body that day instead."

"She was wearing it?"

"No, miss!" He paused and then laughed a little wryly. "We laughed a lot about the way she looked in it. Fitted her all over and touched her nowhere, in a manner of speaking. And the day she died it was fine and sunny. But she would have brought it with her. She knew I needed it out in the bay. She never forgot anything like that, not Miss Linda. . . ." He shook his head. "Maybe she *was* carrying it, but we never found it. I searched for it. Would have liked to keep it after what happened." He looked at me. "You're a lot like Linda Warburton, miss. Taller, now that I look at you. Younger too. But when you said hello, just the way she used to, well. . . ."

I smiled. "I'm sorry, Bob. I'll make sure I don't do that, if I come here again."

"You come whenever you like, miss," he said eagerly. "You want to swim, I'll keep an eye on you, like I used to do for her. Brought her in once when she got caught in a rip. All the Jensen family have been fine swimmers. Swum back from Gibbet myself once when the skiff got holed on a reef. More than a mile! You'll be safe here."

He was beaming at me, fully recovered from his faintness. I smiled and thanked him. I said I'd come again, and meant it. Friendly people were so scarce at Ravensnest that I thought I could understand why Linda Warburton had come here.

But she hadn't been safe. She had fallen to her death from the cliff path.

Climbing, I could see him watching me, his nets forgotten. As I reached the top of the steps I turned and waved to him. He waved an arm in reply and turned back to his net.

"Hello!"

A voice right by my shoulder made me jump and swing round suddenly. Kerr Warburton caught my arm to steady me.

"Why, I'm sorry if I startled you, Diane," he said smoothly. "I thought you'd have seen me."

Pointedly, I disengaged my arm. "I didn't," I said coldly, and thought "and you know damn well I didn't."

"How do you like our beach?" he went on, ignoring my tone of voice. "Not exactly Santa Monica, uh?"

"I like it. It's ... unspoiled, Mr. Warburton."

"My friends call me Kerr," he smiled. He seemed far more assured. Or perhaps that was because his mother was not there. "Are you fond of swimming, Diane?"

"Very," I confessed.

His eyes slid over me, and he nodded. "Yes, you would be. And you look swell in a bikini, I can see that! You should be careful about swimming down at Wreck Beach though. This isn't California. You need to know the currents. We get bad rips off the beach at times. My sister-in-law was carried out down there once. Might have drowned if Jensen hadn't gone in and pulled her out. I suppose you saw the old boy down there? He's the family boatman. Keeps us in fish and lobsters and there isn't a better boatman on the New England coast. All the same, you'd better remember that it isn't safe for a girl like you to go down there alone. Especially if you go swimming."

"I thought Mr. Jensen seemed a very nice man." Which was more than I could say about Kerr Warburton, I decided, flushing beneath his impudent look.

He laughed. "Oh, old Bob's okay! A bit simple perhaps. But he wouldn't harm you. What

I meant was that he might be out at Gibbet when you swim, and no help if you got into trouble. But I'll come down to the beach with you any time you feel like swimming, and keep an eye on you. My wife loathes Wreck Beach, and nobody else at Ravensnest swims there."

I resisted an impulse to tell him that I was quite capable of looking after myself in the water, or on dry land for that matter. I decided it might be more politic to thank him and leave it at that.

"Good!" he said with satisfaction. "Then that's settled. A girl as attractive as you shouldn't be allowed to run around Ravensnest Bay alone."

He moved to take my arm again confidently, but I eluded him.

He laughed. "The shy type, eh? My dear, my interest in you is merely an effort to be friendly. You come from L.A., and you must be used to brightness and life. There isn't much of that around Ravensnest! Still, if you know the right people you can always have fun. That's what I say. I have a car, and I'm the only one at Ravensnest interested enough to use the cruiser down on the slips now that David has buried himself in New York. Did you know there's a roadhouse out past Tregoney, with dancing and music and all the etceteras?"

"Then I suggest you take Mrs. Warburton

there," I said coldly. "I'm sorry, I came to Ravensnest to work—not to play."

He chuckled. "There you go again—I meant *with* Mrs. Warburton, of course. We're the only people near your age at Ravensnest, excepting the servants. It's not a flattering admission, I know. But Daphne isn't jealous of me. She never has been. Sometimes I think Daphne's only interest in me lies in what she expects me to inherit when my mother dies. And now with this new will, I'm afraid she's going to be disappointed. My mother dotes on Robyn. We all know that. And it would be just like Mother to leave the whole estate to her. Like Dickens' characters, the four of us have lived here for most of our lives, putting up with Mother's insults and general bitchery because of our expectations of receiving our rightful shares of the estate one day. By holding that bait in front of our collective nose, she's kept us here as virtually unpaid help. Mother's like that—as you'll find out before long."

"And of course you'd like to know what was in the will, Mr. Warburton?" If Kerr had ever been anyone's unpaid help, the effects were not noticeable.

He nodded eagerly. "Sweetie, that is exactly what I *would* like to know! I happen to be very fond of Daphne. But I also happen to know that she would not stay with me for longer than it took to pack her bags if she thought the old girl had left me nothing."

"Perhaps Mr. Prince could tell you?" I glanced at him obliquely as we walked, and saw his quick flush of anger. But he kept his voice well controlled. He laughed.

"Prince? Prince only jumps the way Martha wants! And you can bet she's sworn him to secrecy. Anyway, he doesn't like Daphne or me. Or Clive and his dear daughter either. Prince is Martha's man, and indirectly that means also David's man. Prince would gloat if Clive and I had to go to work after all these wasted years at Ravensnest."

"Which only leaves your mother," I said. I shook my head sympathetically. "I hardly think she'd tell you anything, Mr. Warburton. At least not while she's in the humor she was in earlier. Do you?"

"I'm goddamn sure she wouldn't!" he exploded. "She's making us all sweat! She knows that, and she's glorying in it!"

That was the truth, I knew. She *was* enjoying it.

"It must be a difficult situation for you, Mr. Warburton."

"Mr. Warburton? Can't you bring yourself to call me Kerr?" he asked curtly.

"I'm afraid I can't," I said. "You see—I only work here as a nurse. And in hospitals nurses are trained to use surnames and courtesy titles."

"Don't expect me to call you Miss Montrose. Diane is what I intend to call you, even when you're angry with me as you seem to be now." He frowned, slowing. We had reached the place where the low stone wall started. Ravensnest lay just ahead. He added: "Ravensnest isn't a hospital, a place of healing. It never has been. It's been anything but. It's known violence and intrigue, and murder."

His hand caught my arm, halting me near the gates where the red brick wall hid us from the house. "Diane, you signed that will. You must have read some of the clauses. I have to know what was in it. I mean that. I have to know! I suppose that old, uh, my mother swore you to secrecy? But what if she did? She's nothing to you! She'll throw you out of Ravensnest first chance. She doesn't want you here, and you can bet she'll go to work on David as soon as she sees him tomorrow. You could be gone from here in a few days. Ravensnest means nothing at all to you. Tell me what you read. I'll make it worth your while, and nobody but you and I need ever know you told me. Five hundred? A thousand? Paid to your bank account wherever you say? Diane. . . ?"

I disengaged my arm carefully. "I'm sorry, Mr. Warburton."

"So she did swear you to secrecy! Diane, I've told you that doesn't matter. You witnessed her signature. You and that Swanson girl from Tregoney. Between you you must have seen most of the will, and no doubt you'll discuss it when you meet, if you haven't already. I saw you with your heads together on the stairs before she left. You've made one enemy here in Martha. Don't make me your enemy too. Just tell me, and the money will go into your account. Talk to Elizabeth Swanson, and find out what she saw. There's a phone in your room. I'll give you till tomorrow."

I looked at him steadily. "If you gave me a year, it could make no difference, Mr. Warburton," I said impatiently. "Mr. Prince covered each sheet of the will carefully before we signed. Even if I wanted to tell you, or Beth wanted to tell you—we couldn't. All we saw were your mother's signatures and our own. You seem to think that everyone is as concerned about the will as you are. Your mother asked me the same thing in a different way. I'm not sure whether she thought I had x-ray eyes, or peeped under Mr. Prince's covering sheets as I signed. But like you, she seemed to think I couldn't resist peeking. Frankly, I couldn't care less what's in the will! I have not the slightest interest in it. I told her that, and I'm telling you. That's the truth, Mr. Warburton. Good afternoon."

My heels tapped angrily as I walked in through the gates, leaving him standing staring after me.

"I think you're lying!" he called after me in a low, angry voice.

I resisted an urge to retort, and kept right on walking.

My anger carried me almost into my own room, before I remembered Robyn. I stopped and looked back. Her door was partly open, and I heard the murmur of voices inside. I hesitated, not wishing to meet Martha Warburton in there right now. But then I heard low, pleasant laughter, and it was a long time since Martha Warburton had laughed like that, I knew.

I tapped, and opened the door gently to see the maid, Molly Waters' startled face look up at me in quick apprehension.

"Miss Montrose! I thought you were Mrs. Rathbone. I just came up to see what Miss Robyn fancied for dinner tonight, and Mrs. Rathbone always says I stay in here too long."

I smiled at her and came in. "And do you, Molly?"

"Well . . . yes, I suppose I do. But you like me to stay for a while, don't you Robyn?"

"Yes," the child said. She glanced apprehensively from Molly to me. "And I asked Daddy could she, and Daddy said yes. Rathbone is a . . . a witch."

Her eyes were gray, I saw. A deep, beautiful gray with the softness of innocence. The blonde hair was not as fair as I had thought, but a golden brown. Her face was faintly flushed in an echo of Molly Waters' consternation at my sudden appearance, and I thought I had never seen a more lovely little girl. But the traces of illness were apparent too, when I looked at her professionally—apparent in the clearness of skin that had an almost transparent quality, and in the bluish shade of cyanosis beneath her eyes and at her lips. She was thin, almost painfully thin, but the frilly little nightgown and bedjacket were designed to disguise it.

I closed the door behind me and smiled at her. "I think you'd be very good for our patient, Molly. She could need someone bright to talk to every now and then. Don't we all?"

"Thank you, Miss Montrose," Molly said, flushing deeper. "I think so too! It's a pity there isn't another child at Ravensnest for her to play with. So sometimes when I'm doing her room, or clearing away her dishes I make up some little game with the dolls and things. Or we bathe them and change their clothes. And she loves it!" she said it defiantly.

"All little girls like games like that," I said. "And even in busy hospitals the nurses try to find time to play with them sometimes. Only of course, in hospitals there are usually a lot of other little girls around to make things interesting. Aren't you going to introduce me to

Robyn, Molly? If we're to be friends, someone should introduce us—don't you think?"

Molly Waters smiled, and touched the child's thin shoulder affectionaly. "Robyn, this is Miss Montrose. She's the nice nurse I told you about, who's come to Ravensnest to look after you. Your father and Mr. Prince found her in Hollywood and asked her to come and look after you."

"In Hollywood?" the child asked wide-eyed. "Where the film stars live? Really in Hollywood?"

I laughed. "Well, not quite in Hollywood, Robyn. But not far away, either. About as far as from Ravensnest to Tregoney, or a little less."

"And you saw some of them?" she looked at me suspiciously with her fine dark brows drawing together. "Did you see Jerry Lewis? Or . . . or Superman?"

I nodded. "Not at the hospital, but driving around Hollywood, or Los Angeles. But I did see a lot of other very famous film stars at the hospital from time to time. You see, even film stars get sick, or hurt themselves and must go to the hospital."

"Will you tell me about them, Miss Montrose?" she asked wide-eyed.

"Of course," I laughed. "Any time, Robyn. Tonight, if you like."

"Tonight? Really?"

"Cross my heart." I said.

"There!" Molly Waters said, smiling. "Didn't I tell you that Miss Montrose was nice? I'll have to go now, or Mrs. Rathbone will have a fit." She straightened and looked at me. "We had another nurse for Robyn once. She used to have dinner in here with her sometimes. She was nice too, wasn't she Robyn? Miss Carruthers. Remember?"

The child nodded, with her bright smile fading. "Rathbone and Grandma sent her away. They won't send you away, will they, Miss Montrose?"

"No," I said quietly. "They won't send me away. Only your father or you can do that, Robyn."

"Then you'll stay a long, long time!" she cried, delighted. " 'Cause I like you, and so will Daddy. And will you have dinner in here with me sometimes, like Miss Carruthers used to?"

"If it can be arranged with Mrs. Rathbone and your grandmother, I don't see why not." I looked at the maid. "What do you think, Molly? Could that be arranged tonight—or will they expect me to eat downstairs?"

"Miss Carruthers used to eat with us in the kitchen," she said considering. "But Mrs. Rathbone didn't say anything about that. Suppose I brought you up a tray when I serve Robyn?"

"Could you?"

She nodded. "I'll bring up a tray. If that isn't

right, they'll tell me quick enough. Dinner is at seven, miss. I usually bring Robyn's dinner up before I have to help Mrs. Rathbone serve for the family."

She smiled and went out, and the child and I looked at one another.

"I said: "You like Molly, don't you, Robyn?"

"Yes," she said gravely. "Molly is cute. But I'm going to like you too, Miss Montrose. I know I am. Even if you do have to give me needles and nasty medicine when Dr. Chester says."

"Do you like Dr. Chester, Robyn?"

"Sure. He brings me candy."

"Then you know he wouldn't ask me to give you medicine, or a needle, unless he was quite sure you needed them to get better."

She nodded. "That's what Grandma says."

"Then your grandmother is a very wise woman."

"Yes. Daddy says she's wise, too. Is it because she's old?"

"Yes, I guess it is." I nodded. "Although some old people are too stubborn, or too foolish to learn from their experiences even if they live to be a hundred."

"Is Grandma like that?" she asked eagerly. "Uncle Kerr and Uncle Clive think so. That's why they don't like her. Uncle Kerr thinks she's mean to everyone at Ravensnest all the time. He says she likes hurting people."

"We should make up our own minds about people, Robyn," I said thoughtfully. "We can't always accept what other people think. We have to learn to think for ourselves. Perhaps your Uncle Clive and Uncle Kerr haven't been nice to her. Has she ever hurt you?"

"No."

"Then you can't think she's mean, can you?"

She shook her head. "I love my grandma. I love her an awful lot, Miss Montrose. Next best to Daddy."

"Then you keep right on doing that," I said, cheerfully. "And maybe you're wiser than Uncle Kerr, or Uncle Clive, or anyone else at Ravensnest."

I smiled at her and ruffled her blonde hair. I was turning when I saw Martha Warburton leaning on her stick at the open door watching us.

"You should not have come in here until you received your instructions from Dr. Chester," she said harshly. "Or at least you should have talked to me. There are things you don't know about Robyn. You could have upset her. You could have made her ill again."

I said quietly: "I don't think anything I've said to Robyn could make her ill, Mrs. Warburton."

Looking at her I could find no anger in her brown eyes, only a deep sadness as she looked at me.

"And what's this about you having dinner with her tonight? Rathbone called me to ask if Waters could bring you a tray in here."

"Robyn is lonely, Mrs. Warburton. She needs company."

"Molly Waters', or yours?" It had a fine edge of sarcasm. She added with her lips twisting slightly: "Of course."

"Or yours, Mrs. Warburton. Preferably yours, I would say. When her father isn't here."

She snorted, disgustedly. "You're here five minutes, and you're trying to run our lives for us! Robyn's and mine. I have to dine downstairs, and everyone at Ravensnest knows that and expects it. I spend what time I can with Robyn."

I nodded. "If you say so, Mrs. Warburton. Excuse me please."

She moved aside, scowling. "I'll tell Rathbone she can send you a tray here tonight. After that you're David's responsibility—not mine. Whether you eat in here with Robyn, with the servants, or with the family will be his decision. Makes no difference to me, one way or the other."

She watched as I walked across the passage to my room and closed the door behind me. Only then I heard her stick tap, and the door closed as she went inside.

She said something to the child in a low voice. Robyn laughed happily.

I stared out the window looking for Wreck Beach, but a jutting headland hid it from me. I could see only the restless green water of Ravensnest Bay, and the slope of Gibbet Island far out.

I glanced down at the sea, and listened, waiting for the hiss of sound that heralded the blowhole's spouting. . . .

CHAPTER

FOUR

I SLEPT BADLY, although the large bed was comfortable and soft, the blankets and eiderdown warm and light. The conflicting characters of the Warburton family kept intruding. When I slept I dreamed, and through my dreams walked the sinister figure of Mrs. Rathbone, the perpetually angry Martha Warburton, the suave Kerr, the frowning Clive.

I woke up sitting bolt upright in bed with my heart pounding heavily in some unknown fright. A new moon like a scimitar hung in my window, and instinct told me that it had been the hiss of the blowhole that had wakened me, though outside my window now all that I could hear was the pounding of the sea at the cliff-face below the courtyard.

I smiled uneasily, and groped on the bedside table for my watch in the cold, keen air. Two-thirty. I yawned in relief. I had not been quite sure where I was. But I was not in a hospital, I was here at Ravensnest, where time was less important. I could go right back to sleep, and stay comfortably asleep for long hours yet. I yawned contentedly, and wriggled down under the clothes again, drawing them up to my chin. In the nurses' home at the hospital any time I had awakened like this it was so close to the time my bedside alarm was due to buzz that it was never worthwhile going back to sleep again.

Momentarily, though, I knew nostalgia for the Los Angeles Medical Center and my friends there. It kept me awake with my heavy-lidded eyes staring at the silver scimitar of moon outside my window. The restless sea seemed to be twice as loud as it had been early in the night. It battered at the stout rock with persistent regularity, as though an angry giant was at work down there, hammering his way towards me, where I lay helpless in the huge bed.

I told myself firmly that I must get used to the sound of the sea outside my window, and that hissing spout of water that I expected again now at any moment. The sooner I came to think of it as a harmless background of night sounds the better. I'd sleep more soundly then, lulled by it. Around me the house of Ravensnest seemed sleeping deeply, contentedly. And I must learn to do the same.

If I started listening for that damned waterspout I knew that I'd still be awake when the sun rose. I turned over on my side and closed my eyes, forcing my mind to be still.

Only suddenly, through the forced quiet, a sound intruded harshly. A fierce, rushing sound, different from any I had heard here before, although my mind at once associated it with the blowhole. But this sound was louder, fiercer, as though something choked that chimney through which the water was forced to rush. I found myself sitting up in bed. I was trembling, and I could feel the skin on the back of my neck building goose pimples that spread slowly down my body beneath my thin nightgown.

Suddenly the sound changed, the hissing became a harsh exploding roar that shook my windows. The scimitar of moon vanished abruptly, obscured by flying spray thrown higher than I would have believed possible. I slid out of bed, shaking with fright. It sounded as though a tidal wave had forced its way into that hidden chamber down there and expelled itself violently through the blowhole.

Tons of water seemed falling back into the

sea and the courtyard below my window. The curtains at my open window flapped and bulged inwards with water dripping from them.

I was poised for flight, staring wide-eyed at the window. I'm not sure what I expected to happen, but I was linking that falling, rushing water with an underwater volcano, or some subterranean upheaval in the Bay of Fundy. I shook at the sound of the giant wave battering its way into the downstairs rooms of Ravensnest, with the whole great house crumbling, falling into ruins like Poe's House of Usher.

But the moon appeared again suddenly in the square of my window, the sound died to a gentle hissing and was gone. Below, the sea seemed gentle and quiet after that moment of fury. I stood still near my bed, trembling, waiting now fearfully for the blowhole to spout again. It took willpower to approach the window and stare out. The heavy curtains were wet beneath my hands, and my bare feet slopped through a pool of seawater that held the icy touch of northern seas.

I stared out apprehensively. With that sliver of moon, I could not see the sea. But the whole window was soaked, and water dripped everywhere around me.

I fumbled at the window, closing it. I retreated to my bed and stood beside it waiting. The spout seemed a long time coming again. A very long time. Minutes passed, each an hour, with the only sound in my room the muted roll of the waves and the steady thumping of my heart.

I heard it start abruptly, and tensed. But it was no longer angry, or roaring with suppressed energy. It was a familiar deep hiss, as it had been in the afternoon, I heard the water rise, and knew that its apex had not even reached the level of the courtyard paving below. I listened to it fall almost gently back into the sea.

And suddenly a new horror touched me. *Something* had blocked the chimney! That had been the reason for the frightening roar of sound I had heard. That had been the reason for that column of water thrown so high that it reached my window and drenched the whole easterly wall of Ravensnest.

It must have sounded like that once when the wreckers had locked some poor sailor in the cell in the cliff, and the sea had forced his body up the chimney and flung it back into the sea, expelling it like a cork from a wine bottle through the chimney by the mighty pressure of wave and tide. . . .

I leaped back into bed and pulled up the clothes. I lay shivering, and wishing I'd never left Los Angeles. For the moment I was a frightened girl again, cowering in the dark. It was a long time before training and intelligence reasserted themselves, and I reasoned that it did not have to be a body that had caused the blockage. That it would have been some flotsam of the sea forced inside, to choke the chimney temporarily until it was expelled.

But it was a long time before I could sleep. . . .

I woke up heavy-eyed. I stared, fighting sleep. It was morning and bright sunshine was flooding the room as someone drew the curtains aside, and opened my windows. I saw the neat maid's uniform with relief as memory of the night came back to me.

"Good morning, Miss Montrose."

Molly Waters smiled at me as she came back from the window, and I could smell the fragrance of coffee somewhere close.

I yawned and sat up, stretching. "Hello, Molly."

"I brought you some morning coffee when I brought up Robyn's hot milk. Did you sleep well?"

I managed to smile as I remembered last night's disturbance. "Up to a point. The blowhole made an awful racket and wakened me. I found it hard to get back to sleep. Did you hear it?"

She shook her head, smiling. "It worried me too at first. But you get used to it. After a while you just don't hear it half the time, waking or sleeping."

"This one should have wakened the dead," I said. "It sounded like an atom bomb! It blew water into the room. Didn't you notice the wet curtains? And there's a pool of water by the windows. That's why I closed them. Surely you heard it?"

"No." She looked at me curiously. Almost as though she suspected me of dreaming it. "But the curtains are damp. I'll clean them later. The salt often stains them. But mostly the water that gets into the upstairs rooms is just flying spray, very fine. The heavy curtains and the carpet sop it up quickly." She smiled at me, and colored slightly as she confessed, "I sleep like a log. Never move once I go to bed. And Ken and I are dating. We went into Tregoney last night to see a film. Perhaps it was while I was away?"

I smiled, remembering Ken Bryant's pleasant young face. "Not unless you stayed out late. It was around half past two. And it sounded more like an explosion than just water spurting up."

She frowned. "Maybe something got stuck in there? It does, you know. Though I've never known the water to reach this window before except once."

I lowered my voice instinctively. "That is exactly how it sounded to me, Molly. As though something was stuck in there and had to be forced out. Tell me about the time it reached this window before. Was that long ago? Did you hear it?"

She nodded. "Yes, I heard it. So did Ken. It was just frightening. It woke the both of us, though Mrs. Rathbone didn't hear it. It was late at night, and it was two years ago. I remember, because it was the next day that poor Mrs. David Warburton was killed. I thought afterwards it seemed like an omen. Like something bad would happen to someone at Ravensnest. But of course, that's silly. Mrs Rathbone told me that it sometimes happens that way, that the outlet from the secret room get blocked up with kelp after heavy seas. Ken has to go down there and clean it sometimes at low tide. He's supposed to keep it free of rubbish. Once he found a plank jammed down there, and had to get it out. But mostly it's just kelp. I suppose he's forgotten to clean it lately. He has plenty of other things to do. Mrs. Rathbone keeps us all busy. You won't speak about it to her? Ken would be in trouble."

"I won't say anything to Mrs. Rathbone," I promised, relieved. Of course. That was what it must have been. Kelp.

She smiled at me. "Have you heard about how they used the secret room? They were wreckers once. They used to lock the survivers from the wrecks in the room. They drowned in there, and the water forced their bodies out and threw them back into the sea. When the bodies floated up again, they recovered them and buried them on Gibbet Island. They said they'd been drowned in the wreck. And the bodies had no wounds. At least, that's what the people in Tregoney say. Mrs. Rathbone says it's all lies. She says only one of the Warburtons was a bad man. Nathan. He was a pirate."

I nodded. "I heard about that. Beth Swanson told me. Which story do you believe, Molly?"

She glanced at the door nervously. "My grandfather used to tell us tales that'd make your hair stand, Miss Montrose. He had them from his grandfather. There's bad blood in the Warburtons. And it didn't end when sail went out either! Take a look at all the ships' logs in the library, you know, the diaries of the voyage that ships' captains keep. It was supposed to be fair enough to loot a wrecked ship. But to lure a ship onto the Gibbet Island reefs with false lights, and kill the survivors—that was something different. That was murder!"

"But that's old hat now, Molly."

"Uhuh," she said. "*They* say it never happened. And those old dead will never come back to challenge that now. But they're a queer lot still, the Warburtons. I can put up with Martha's tantrums. But Kerr and Clive. . . ? They give me the creeps."

"Martha can't be of Warburton blood? She only married a Warburton."

"But you're wrong there," Molly Waters said

86

quickly. "She married her cousin. You should drink your coffee, Miss Montrose. It gets cold fast here. Breakfast is at eight, and Mrs. Rathbone said you are to have it with us in the kitchen this morning. The others don't come down for breakfast often. Mr. David is expected at eleven."

"Thanks Molly. What about Dr. Chester?"

"Nobody ever knows what time Dr. Chester will turn up. But you'll hear his car no doubt."

Revived by the coffee I showered and dressed. Time enough to put on a uniform again when I had to, I decided. Street clothes are a luxury to a nurse, and not to be discarded lightly.

I went into Robyn, and helped her bathe and get back into bed. Dr. Chester had left a page of instruction for Robyn's medicines, and when Molly brought up the child's cereal and fruit juice I persuaded Molly to allow me to give her the morning ritual dosage, establishing our first real nurse-patient relationship so that I'd be better prepared to talk to Dr. Chester when he came.

I checked her pulse and temperature automatically, but to satisfy my own curiosity rather than for Dr. Chester, who had left no instruction about that, to me, important detail. There was a slight fever, that seemed to be chronic if I went by a couple of scrawled notations on Dr. Chester's instruction sheet. Her pulse was weak and rather fast. These were things that I filed in my mind for future reference. We made rather a joke of it between us, and she seemed to like me fussing around her.

Afterwards I wandered along the passage, turning the corner of David Warburton's suite. Most of the rooms farther on were locked on the outside, so presumably unoccupied. But I discovered a stairway leading back beneath the passage directly down into the courtyard beneath my window. A door stood open down there, and I could hear someone whistling cheerfully. I glanced at my watch. Half an hour to breakfast yet.

It was dark on the narrow stairway, and I blinked when I stepped out hesitantly into bright sunshine. Two white-painted seats that I couldn't see from my window stood against the red brick wall, and Ken Bryant was busy cleaning the lower windows, a bucket of soapy water and cloths beside him while he polished energetically.

He saw me, and grinned. His whistling stopped on a high note.

"Good morning, Miss Montrose!" he said pleasantly.

"Good morning, Ken."

"The windows on this side are always thick with salt. Clean them this morning, and by tomorrow it has to be done again. The salt crusts on the stone flags too, and I have to hose it off all the time."

"The blowhole seemed to be blocked last night," I said. "It made a noise like a cannon in clearing itself, and threw salt water right up into my room. Maybe that's why the walls are so wet this morning. Didn't you hear it?"

He glanced guiltily at the kitchen door. "I didn't hear anything. But it's that goddamn kelp! It gets forced in at high tide and blocks the vent." He put down his cloth. "I'd better go down and take a look right away. Why they keep a room like that I'll never know. Mr. David would have got rid of it long ago—but the others seem to think it's an attraction to guests. Everyone wants to see it."

"I'd like to see it myself," I admitted.

He glanced at me. "Not much to see. Just a room cut in the solid rock. It's always damp and slippery, and stinks of rotting kelp most of the time. Or fish that get themselves stranded inside. There used to be old leg-irons and things down there, but they've rusted away. But if you want to look, come down with me now. Once is enough to see it." He glanced at me inquiringly.

I nodded. "I'd like to see it, Ken. But is there time before breakfast?"

"Plenty of time. Come on. It will only take ten minutes. But I'll need a flashlight. Wait here. . . ." He came back grinning. "Got it. Let's take a look at Ravensnest's chamber of horrors."

"Do you believe those old stories, Ken?" I asked nervously as I followed him towards what looked like a small stone room that backed against the protective wall.

"Why not?" he said, glancing at me. "People don't build a place like it just to look at, Miss Montrose. Oh, it was used all right. And often enough too. They used to say it was haunted once."

"By the ghosts of seamen?"

"Not exactly seamen. One ship wrecked on Gibbet was an immigrant ship from England. They say one lifeboat reached Wreck Beach. It was packed with people. They all went back to the sea through the secret room. There were women and children in it as well as men, but that didn't worry the wreckers. Knew an old guy in Tregoney who swore he'd heard their ghosts wailing on moonlight nights while he was fishing in Ravensnest Bay. They would have had plenty of time for wailing, if they'd been locked in at low tide. The guy was a bit queer in the head though—so I guess all he heard was seabirds."

He was removing a heavy wooden bar from iron sockets at the back of the entrance chamber. Below me I could hear the sea as he opened a heavy wooden door on protesting hinges.

"Locks are no good, of course," he muttered. "Too much salt. So we use bars of oak, and oaken doors here and below. They have to be renewed every fifty years or so, they say; though they haven't been changed in the time of anyone at Ravensnest, unless it's Mrs. Warburton Senior. Better go down carefully, it gets slippery, even up here. I'll go first and shine the flashlight. . . ."

I followed him gingerly. The steps were of stone, and it was pitch black inside the door. The steps led down steeply. It was like descending into a slanting well cut in solid stone. My mind pictured the flaring torches of resinous wood, the glinting arms of wreckers forcing trembling captives down the very steps I was treading.

"Wouldn't it have been easier to just throw them from the cliffs?"

He laughed. "I guess so! But some might have fought back. This way there were no marks of violence on the bodies. When they fished them from the sea again who could say they hadn't died in the wreck? At least that's the story." He stopped and flashed his flashlight on the rock wall. It steadied on a worn, horizontal mark grooved deeply. "That's the height the great spring tides reach," he said. "It's six feet above the roof of the cell. The present door isn't as tight as it should be, some water gets around it. You'll find the steps very slippery now. But the door is just ahead, and it's lighter inside. Light comes in through the water channels as you'll see."

I slipped and braced myself. I followed him down like a cat walking on ice.

I held the flashlight for him while he removed another great beam, and then a second and a third that sat in heavy iron sockets.

"The door sticks," he muttered, straining at it. "You get too much kelp inside and it's goddamn hard to open!"

He gave a final heave and the door opened partly. He took the flashlight from me and squeezed inside. I could hear him kicking kelp away and swearing. The door opened at last protestingly. I had never seen a door as thick. It was built of what looked like solid oak at least a foot thick.

"One of these days it's going to stick fast," he said. "And that will be that! Someone will have to blast it open with explosives, I guess. I hope they blast the whole goddamn cell down into the sea."

"Is there water in there?" I asked anxiously.

"No. Just wet kelp. It's low tide now. Mind holding the flashlight?"

I held the flashlight while he kicked the kelp into heaps and thrust it over against the far wall. Light filtered faintly into a stone cell, light with the green-brown of kelp that he was thrusting into floor-level channels that sloped down towards the sea outside. The kelp moved wetly, and I could hear it sliding down. Water swished and gurgled in the channels as the kelp freed.

"Sometimes we go months without any kelp at all in here," said Ken. "But in the summer storms it comes in thick. We had a storm here last week." He cleared the last of it. "You can come in now."

I joined him, and stared around curiously. There wasn't much to see. Green seaweed grew on the walls. The roof was an inverted funnel and the floor was slippery enough to be dangerous. After the stories I had heard, seeing the secret room was anticlimactic. It was just a cell cut in rock, shaped like a chimney. It smelled of rotting kelp and the sea—a damp, unpleasant smell that I wanted to leave behind me.

Ken Bryant flashed his light up into the funnel-shaped hole.

"They had good stonemasons in those days. How they cut this I'll never know. It slopes into a pipe the diameter of a man's shoulders, and there's ten feet or more of it to the air topside. Takes a lot of kelp to choke it. Well, it's clear now. Must have cleared last night the way you said. Come over here and I'll show you."

I stared up at the bright sunlight above, and examined the inlet channels. There were five of them in the outer wall below water level, and I could see the light filtering through the moving water with an eerie effect. I shuddered, picturing myself locked in here, waiting for the tide, the rush of water forced up those channels by succeeding waves. . . .

"I want to go back now," I said hastily.

Ken laughed. "Sure. Everyone does. But it's safe enough at low tide. See this rusted iron? There used to be leg-irons fastened to it once. Maybe they thought some of the men might try to worm their way up the chimney. Not much chance though, unless they were dwarfs. Well, back to my windows. And your breakfast will be about ready. . . ."

I left him barring the great oak door, and climbed up gingerly. It was a long time since I had been as glad to see the sun again and breathe in the sea air. I stepped gratefully out into the courtyard and walked to the stone wall to stare down curiously. I discovered the open end of the vent, now that I knew where to look for it. It could have been one of the many holes down there above sea level eroded in the rock. I searched for other evidence of the secret room, but could find none. If the entrance to the stairway had been hidden well in those days, the death cell would indeed have been a secret one.

I pictured the mass of kelp thrown high last night, the rising waterspout, the kelp and seawater falling back into the sea. I could see some of it left on the rocks by the receding tide.

Farther down in the water something dark moved as a wave broke and receded. I froze suddenly, hearing Ken Bryant barring the door near me.

Something dark had moved in the water, something caught amongst the rocks, something that spread two arms wide in protest against the rushing water. I was close to fainting. That was a body down there beneath the water. I was sure of it. I could see the two arms, the bulk of the torso distorted by water. . . .

"Ken! Ken. . . !" I screamed.

He came over, and saw my face and stopped abruptly. "What is it, Miss Montrose? Are you ill?" he asked anxiously, his quick smile gone.

"There's a . . . a body down there!" I muttered sickly. "In the water. It must have been thrown out of the cell last night, when—"

He joined me quickly, staring down. "I don't see anything."

"There!" I said, pointing. "Between the two big rocks in deep water. It's not far out from the blowhole. You'll see it when the next wave breaks and runs back. *There. See it?*"

He started, staring down intently.

It's a body," I mumbled. "It has . . . no head!"

The wall I was gripping felt as though it moved.

"It has a head *now*." he muttered. "But God—it can't be—?"

"Someone must have been in there last

night," I mumbled in horror. "Locked in! Waiting...."

"No." he said. "It's not a body. It's...?" He broke off. He started to laugh. "Look again, Miss Montrose," he chuckled. "For a moment you had me believing it *was* a body. It's that goddamn secret room down there. It does things to you. Look again. It's just an old slicker with a hood. Like fishermen wear. Someone must have thrown it away, or lost it overboard. You can see it plainly now. That's all it is. An old slicker...."

The arms still spread wide. It was caught by the hem. I could see the head bobbing like dead lead now—but the coat had opened wide, and it was empty. As I watched it freed itself. A wave rushing in rolled it up and slid it into deeper water and it was gone.

I let my breath sigh out in relief, and met Ken Bryant's amused eyes. But he looked relieved too.

"It sure looked like a body," he chuckled. "I'll give you that. Had me scared for a minute, all black and with its arms spread. I guess it scared you plenty too, eh Miss Montrose?"

"It did indeed!" I admitted with feeling.

But I was remembering suddenly as I went back into the house that fisherman Bob Jensen had talked about a slicker like that. A slicker that Linda Warburton had worn the day she died. I shook off the thought. Linda Warburton had been dead for two years. The slicker must have rotted away long since. Nothing would have been left of it by now. Nothing. . . .

CHAPTER

FIVE

KEN BRYANT HAD said that I could expect to hear Dr. Chester's car when he arrived at Ravensnest. I did. It was ten years old at least, and the coastal roads had taken a toll of its usefulness. It rattled, and had a loose muffler, so that it sounded like a racing car escaped from Daytona, even though its best speed seemed to be about thirty.

And like his car, Dr. Chester also was past his prime. His hair was a startling white through which a cherubic pink scalp showed. He was plump, and all pink and white, and he had extremely faded blue eyes that peered at Robyn short-sightedly through thick bifocals. His suit was old-fashioned, the trousers too wide, and driving had left it looking as though he had slept in it.

But he joked cheerfully with Robyn, and found a packet of candy in his pocket for her, which she accepted gravely, and promptly hid beneath her pillow very carefully while they exchanged winks in what I guessed was a ritual between them.

He was, I supposed, fairly typical of older generation G. P.'s in a place like Tregoney, Maine: a family doctor who made friends of his patients, and even if he was not able to keep up with the most modern procedures, at least gave them the encouragement of his personal optimism and sympathy. And that, I knew, was a practice rapidly falling into disuse among the younger doctors. Mostly in the hospitals that kind of sympathetic encouragement had to come from nurses, if at all. The doctors were noncommittal, prescribed their miracle drugs and went on their calm way. There was no time to make friends of patients, and most believed that it was not a good thing anyway.

However, I decided that I liked Dr. Chester. Though I had to admit that I was not quite sure whether that liking was for the doctor or the man. He talked constantly as he examined her.

"I suppose you think we should have a chart hanging at the head of Robyn's bed, Miss Montrose, eh? Like they do in the hospitals you've worked around? Well, maybe I'll leave you a spring clip and some sheets of ruled paper to fill in, and you can keep her statistics for me, eh? No point in doing that before. Nobody here with enough *nous* to do it for me. I suppose you know that Robyn has rheumatic fever?"

"No, Doctor. Mrs. Warburton said that you'd explain everything to me when you called."

"Hmm. Rheumaticky lot, the Warburtons. Eh, Rob? Even Grandma Martha has it. Comes of living on top of the sea for generations, I suppose. Robyn needs bed rest for six months, and only two of those months gone this time, which leaves four to go. There's some carditis, Miss Montrose, so she needs careful nursing, and no strains or stresses. Want you to keep a record of her temperature twice a day for me. She has pain in her knees, ankles and wrists. Flits around the large joints. I've been treating the pain with aspirin. Bed rest and diet help some. We keep her bowel movements regular. She gets eight grains of aspirin every four hours. I hope to be able to halve that soon. It's . . . you tell her, Rob!"

"It's a grain for each year of my life, Miss Montrose. I'm eight."

"The main object in treating Robyn's complaint is to avoid cardiac complications," Dr. Chester said cheerfully. "Chronic valvular disease is something we don't want around the place. Martha has it, and one's enough! Absolute rest in bed from the start with careful nursing is the way to prevent that. Any time you catch her sweating, you wrap her in a blanket instead of her sheet. Know anything about Sydenham's chorea?"

"Yes, Doctor," I said, startled.

"Well, you watch for early symptoms. You see them, call me right away. Not that I can do much in the way of urgent treatment for that, since treatment is the same as what she's getting now. But I'd like to know."

The child looked up at him, frowning. "What's . . . chorea, Dr. Chester?"

He chuckled. "Well, it's a complication of what you have Rob; I doubt that you'll ever get it. We've been looking after you too well. But Miss Montrose will know. Another doctor once said that a choreic child is punished three times before her condition is recognized. Once for fidgeting, once for breaking her dishes, and once for making faces at her grandma."

He wasn't laughing, though, as he looked at me. Sydenham's chorea was not a joking matter. It was a disease of the brain that affected children, and one closely allied to the rheumatic fever for which he was treating Robyn Warburton. Involuntary movements, grimaces, twitching, inability to grasp a cup or a plate were usually the first unnoticed symptoms, so

101

his humorous remark had a very real significance. I found it appropriate, though it was a simplification I hadn't heard before.

He said as we walked outside into the passage: "I suppose you've seen plenty of rheumatic fever cases in the childrens' wards?"

"Yes, Doctor."

"Didn't keep them there long though, eh? Needed the beds."

I frowned. "They used to say that the mortality was low. And the beds *were* always needed."

"The immediate mortality of rheumatic fever is low, but it takes a heavy toll in deaths from cardiac failure later in life, Miss Montrose," he said grimly. "*And* it's a disease that recurs. The chances of relapse during the first year after the first attack are high. So we have to have careful nursing and care for that first year. This is Robyn's first year. That's why you're here. I'd like to move Robyn away from Ravensnest. But that isn't possible unless David marries again. If he should, I'd advise him to live somewhere inland with her for a year or so. Away from the sea, and cold and chills. Well, maybe he will one day soon. Matter of finding the right woman, I guess. Thought a lot of his wife. Let's go look at Martha."

I smiled, "I'm afraid Mrs. Warburton Senior doesn't like the idea of a nurse at Ravensnest.

She may resent it if I walk into her room with you, Doctor."

"Let me handle that old battle-axe," he said. "Martha isn't as fierce as she sounds. Well, not quite anyway."

But I noticed that he hesitated outside her door briefly, and that he knocked gently.

"Who's there?" her harsh voice demanded.

"Dr. Chester, Martha."

"Expect me to open the door for you? You know your way in."

I followed him inside. She lay in her clothes on a couch near the window and her eyes flicked to me at once, coldly hostile. "What's she doing in here?"

"Now Martha," he said placatively. "I've been telling you for years that you need a nurse. And Miss Montrose is a good one."

"For Robyn maybe. But neither you nor that son of mine are going to prescribe any nurse for me, Kenneth!"

He grinned at her rising wrath calmly enough. "And you're not a child? Sure, I know that, Martha. You're an aging woman, and crippled with rheumatoid arthritis right now. Rathbone has to undress you at night, and dress you in the mornings. And Rathbone has to give you your injections. Right?"

She sniffed. "You know she does. And do most everything else but eat and drink for me. So what? I pay her for it."

"And every time we talk about Rathbone and what she does for you, you tell me she's as clumsy as a longshoreman with two left feet and a skinful of rotgut, and that she hurts you every time she touches you. Right?"

"So what? D'you think I'd let Kerr's wife or that fool Isabel do things for me?"

"Nope," Dr. Chester said cheerfully. "Miss Montrose, lift her for me will you? Put some cushions behind her and make her comfortable till we take a look at her."

"Yes, Doctor."

She glared at me as I gathered cushions that she had thrown carelessly from the couch. "Don't you dare touch me, Montrose."

"Can you get up yourself, Mrs. Warburton?" I asked mildly, the cushions within reach. I sensed Dr. Chester watching from where he had opened his bag on the table.

"Of course I can!"

But she winced with pain when she moved, and I heard her quick breath, and saw the agony grow nakedly in her eyes as she struggled to get up, but could not.

I said: "It's really quite easy to move a patient without hurting them, or straining anything. If you like I'll show Mrs. Rathbone how it's done. . . ."

I think I had her raised and positioned before she realized what I was doing. I felt resistance come, stiffening her muscles, but it was

104

too late. I was already holding her gently, making the cushions more comfortable before I laid her back. She winced as her stiffened muscles relaxed.

"You should relax your muscles more, Mrs. Warburton," I said gently. "Leave everything to your nurse. I know how painful inflamed joints can be, and stiffness and resistance aggravates the pain."

"She's right about that, Martha," Dr. Chester said heartily, coming over with his stethoscope. "Well, well. She's got you up already. She hurt you as much as Rathbone does?"

"No," she admitted grudgingly. "She's younger, stronger maybe."

"And hurt you less, eh?" He glanced at me and winked. "I think I'll have to ask you to give Mrs. Warburton her needle today, Miss Montrose. Got a little of Mrs. Warburton's own trouble in the joints of my right hand. You'll find the hypodermic in my bag. Spirits, and an ampule of ACTH. Intramuscular. The deltoid for preference. She's on a five-weeks' course of the hormone. Would have started her on it sooner if I'd known she was going to walk around the house yesterday remaking her fool will."

"Made no difference if you had. And you needn't think I'm going to let this woman stick needles into me. What d'you think I pay *you* for?"

"For knowing how it should be done, and what to look for afterwards," he said, grinning at her.

But he was not as casual as he sounded, and I was glad of that. The administration of ACTH, intramuscularly, is a chore the attending doctor rather than the nurse should carry out. But I prepared the needle, choosing a new and sharp one, and bared her thin arm despite her defiant glare. The skin was toughened and scarred from other needle marks over a long period.

He watched closely, checking the ampule of ACTH, and the needle. Because of the relatively greater blood supply of the muscles, drugs injected intramuscularly are absorbed more quickly than those given subcutaneously. Most doctors seem to prefer the deltoid or triceps muscle of the upper arm for their injections, but with Mrs. Warburton this was no large area, and already there seemed too much scarring. I decided that it would be a lot easier for both of us if she had the injections in her buttocks. I made up my mind to ask Dr. Chester about that at the first opportunity.

I cleansed the withered, toughened skin with alcohol, and inserted the needle with a quick thrust at right angles through the skin into the muscle. I aspirated gently to make sure that the needle hadn't entered a vessel. When no blood showed, I injected the ACTH without incident.

"They trained you well at Los Angeles, Miss Montrose," Chester said with satisfaction. "Couldn't have given that one better myself. How was it, Martha? Hurt you any more than usual?"

Martha Warburton flexed her arm gingerly and glared at him. "What do you mean, you couldn't have given it better? Any time you give me a needle, Kenneth, it feels like you're using a hammer and a blunt ice pick. She didn't hurt me—but that doesn't mean I need a nurse. I pay *you* to treat me. Any time I want a change I'll get myself another doctor, not a nurse."

"And I'd let you do that, if I thought there was any other doctor in the area fool enough to come out here to you most every day," Chester snorted. "Martha, I've more patients than a man of my age should be expected to look after. And a lot of them need me far worse than you do. If cortisone is going to be any help to you, it has to be given to you regularly, and exactly as prescribed. And there has to be someone around you with the experience and know-how to watch for side effects. I can't spend all my time here listening to you working off your spite, even if I wanted to."

"Why you old. . . !" Her color predicted imminent explosion.

"What you've got, you've had for long enough to learn to live with it," he said as though he hadn't heard. "And looking after you is about the most thankless chore I've discovered in nearly forty years of medicine. You need Miss Montrose, whether you like the idea of not. And any time I can't make it out here because I have someone who really needs my help, she can give you these injections. If you start to react unfavorably to the cortisone, she has the training to recognize your symptoms and report it to me at once. I can then order corrective treatment which she can carry out until I get here. . . ."

"Hah!" she said disdainfully. "So you're not even sure yourself about this newfangled treatment you're giving me."

"You're going to have a nurse, Martha," he said grimly. "You're going to have a trained nurse in attendance on you here, or I'm going to advise young David to have you put in a hospital or a nursing home where you can be taken care of effectively."

"That's what you think," she snapped. "I'm still mistress of Ravensnest!"

"What have you got against Miss Montrose?"

She glanced at me where I was cleansing the hypodermic and placing it in alcohol. She sniffed. "Who said I've anything against the girl? I've nothing against her. But neither you nor that son of mine can make me do anything I don't want to do. And neither can she."

"There's no reason in you, Martha. You're acting like a spoiled child!"

"I could say the same of you, Kenneth Chester. Except that you're acting more like a mule."

While they glared at one another I heard footsteps outside Martha Warburton's door, and someone knocked gently.

"See who that is, Miss Montrose!" Chester snapped.

I walked over and opened the door. "Yes?"

A man stood in the doorway, the beginnings of a smile on his lips. He was tall and strongly built with the powerful shoulders of a footballer; his eyes were very dark and his hair the glossy-black of the Warburtons. I knew at once that this must be David Warburton, for the family resemblance was strong, but there was no malice in his face. Only a touch of sadness around his eyes.

He kept his eyes on my face; the half-smile faded and I knew that he too must have seen my resemblance to his wife.

"Mr. Warburton?" I smiled gently. "I'm Diane Montrose, the nurse Mr. Prince engaged for you."

"Nurse?" He recovered his poise. "Oh, of course. I'm sorry, Miss . . . Montrose, is it?"

"Ah, David." Dr. Chester interrupted. "Come in. About time you were here. This is Miss Diane Montrose, our new nurse, and a good one too, I might add. Miss Montrose, this is Robyn's father."

He followed me into the room and held out his hand. "Welcome to Ravensnest." His grip was firm and quick. "I've just come from Robyn. She likes you very much. I hope you'll stay with us for a long while."

"She'd be gone already if Martha had her way," snorted Dr. Chester. "For Pete's sake, David, come and talk some sense into this mother of yours. She's being twice as difficult as usual."

David walked over and kissed his mother, patting her shoulder gently.

"Miss Montrose," Dr. Chester said quietly. "Would you mind taking the syringe and needles down to the kitchen for sterilization? Ten minutes please."

"Yes Doctor. . . ."

Behind me as I went out I heard David Warburton say calmly. "Now what's all this, Mother? She seems a nice girl, and Robyn likes her. And Dr. Chester says he needs someone with you while you're having cortisone treatment. . . ."

I was glad to escape into the passage. The house around me was quiet and cool. Outside the front porch an expensive European sedan stood on the gravel drive near Dr. Chester's old car. It gleamed in black enamel thinly coated with dust, its upholstery red morocco leather. A jaguar mascot sprang forward from the hood.

I sighed and turned towards the kitchen, and

saw Clive Warburton coming along the passage towards me carrying a newspaper in his hand.

"Good morning, Miss Montrose. Was that David went upstairs just now?" The white lock of hair gave him an almost satanic look as his brown eyes probed mine.

"Yes. He's with Mrs. Warburton Senior and Dr. Chester."

He glanced at the enamel receptacle in my hands, and smiled. "Got rid of you, eh?" He came closer. "I suppose Kerr asked you about my cousin's will? You wouldn't know what was in it, of course?"

"I witnessed signatures, Mr. Warburton. That was all," I said coldly. "As I told your nephew, each page was covered while we witnessed Mrs. Warburton's signature."

"Prince would see to that." He nodded, studying me. "And the same applied when Beth Swanson signed?"

"Yes."

"I told that fool nephew of mine that was the way it would be." He frowned, still barring my way, his dark eyes studying me with an almost malevolent gleam. "When people insist on secrecy—in my experience they have something to hide. Something they're ashamed of. Wouldn't you say that the Warburton estates should belong to the Warburton family, and not to any one person, Miss Montrose?"

111

"I really couldn't say, Mr. Warburton. It's no business of mine. I. . . ."

He nodded. "You merely came here to nurse, huh?"

I said stiffly: "That's right."

"Okay," he shrugged, then went on. "And what's this I hear about you going down into the secret room this morning with young Bryant?" He contrived to make it sound as though I'd done something underhand.

I reddened indignantly. "Well, if I wasn't supposed to go down there someone should have told me. The blowhole made such a racket last night that I couldn't sleep. It sounded like a bomb exploding. Bryant went down to clear the kelp that he thought must have choked it. I was curious because of that, and because until I came here torture chambers were new to me!"

"It was not a torture chamber, you know," he said. "It was a place of execution. A place for swift and painless death when the water flooded."

"And while the poor wretches waited? Waiting wasn't torture?"

"Contrary to popular belief, Miss Montrose, they did not have to wait. In those days there were heavy iron traps that closed the inlets. They were raised from above by ropes and pulleys. The water didn't rise slowly with the tide. It poured in in a flood. And until the traps were raised to let the water in, I doubt that any of the victims suspected. They were given rum to lull their fears. And they were given light. They thought they had escaped the sea, and were grateful."

I frowned. "You seem to have made a study of it. Everyone else denies it ever happened."

He nodded. "As you say, I have made a study of it. I have a curious nature, and some of our ancestors left papers, diaries that make certain things clear enough to me. Why deny the truth? These things happened. And the Warburtons were not the only wreckers on this coast, Miss Montrose. Bryant told me you saw an old slicker down there in the water this morning? Is that so?"

I shivered involuntarily, remembering. "Yes. There was a . . . a raincoat with a hood down there, caught amongst the rocks. It looked like . . . a body."

"So Bryant said. You saw it clearly, of course?"

"Yes, we both did." I remembered what Bob Jensen had said again suddenly, but decided not to mention that. I merely added: "It couldn't have been in the sea for long. It hadn't rotted. Bryant thought it might have fallen from some fishing boat out in the bay."

"He also thought that it might have been driven into the secret room, and blocked the outlet last night to make the roar of sound that disturbed you."

"Yes, he did. And so did I."

His rather sensuous lips curled briefly, and he smiled at me and stood aside.

"You were both wrong, Miss Warburton. The slicker was mine."

I stared at him. "Yours, Mr. Warburton?"

"I have a room not far from yours. The coat had mildewed, and I cleaned it and put it on the window ledge to dry yesterday morning. I'm afraid I forgot about it. It must have blown down into the sea. It was an old one, so that does not matter. I'm sorry it frightened you."

I frowned. "I was not afraid, Mr. Warburton," I lied. "Just curious. But you must excuse me, I have to sterilize these things for Dr. Chester."

I walked past him and went to the kitchen. As I closed the kitchen door behind me, he was still standing in the passage with the newspaper in his hand, looking after me.

CHAPTER
SIX

I FOUND A sullen, but slightly more accepting Martha Warburton when I returned from sterilizing Dr. Chester's hypodermic. David Warburton was visiting with Robyn, and I could hear their low voices in her room as I passed by performing routine chores set by Dr. Chester.

He had instructed me to use what in hospitals was normal follow-up during long-term cortisone therapy. Martha Warburton must now be checked carefully at regular intervals and her response to the therapy noted. The simple clinical observations and tests were designed to help us notice the beginning of any adverse side effect, which with cortisone is always possible. So I must check her weight and blood pressure, her urine for sugar and question her about any gastrointestinal pain or discomfort.

She came to accept my presence and the things I did, with only an occasional biting comment. She would have had to be a fool not to prefer the carefully chosen needles I used, and the hospital technique of administration to Dr. Chester's fumbling with stiffened fingers and blunt needles, for I quickly found he would use a needle until he had to practically drive it in like a nail before he would discard it for a new one. Dr. Chester counted his pennies.

David, I was to find quickly, was easy to work with. And Robyn adored her father. While he was at Ravensnest, I did not need to concern myself with the little girl's loneliness. He gave her every minute of his time that he could spare.

When it came to dinner that first Saturday night I was not sure what to do, but Molly Waters brought up my dinner to Robyn's room as she had the previous night. And as I had done then, I changed my simple white uniform for a dress, dressing up as much for my own morale as for the child's. I used makeup, and was careful with my hair, though I could not have put into words why I thought so much trouble necessary. It had been a hard day. Not hard by hospital standards, but a day full of unexpected tensions that had taken their toll of nervous energy.

With Robyn I started to relax. We had formally invited two of her dolls to dinner, and she was laughing merrily when I heard the rumble of a traymobile outside and someone knocked. David Warburton came in, followed by a smiling Molly Waters wheeling his dinner, with a tall, slim bottle of wine protruding from a bucket of ice, and covered savory dishes.

"Do you two people mind if I join you?" his deep, pleasant voice asked humorously. "Or am I interrupting a little private dinner party?"

I looked around at him, smiling. "Not at all," I said, turning quickly to smile at him. "I'm sure Robyn would be delighted. . . ." I broke off abruptly.

He had stopped, staring at me, as both Clive Warburton and Bob Jensen had. His face was pale, almost jaundiced beneath his tan. Molly almost ran into him with the tray, and he muttered something and moved aside, starting to frown at me.

"Is something the matter, Mr. Warburton?" I asked anxiously, "Are you ill?"

He shook his head. "No. I'm okay, Miss Montrose. Something . . . surprised me, that's all."

I left Robyn and walked over to him.

"It's okay," I said softly. "I understand. I went down to Wreck Beach yesterday and gave poor Bob Jensen an awful fright. He told me about . . . that I looked very like your wife.

117

Would you rather have dinner alone with Robyn? It's quite all right. I can take mine across the passage to my room. I. . . ."

His color was coming back slowly. His frown faded. He shook his head. "Please stay!" he said quickly. "It was just that you looked so like her for the moment. The dress, and the way you smiled at me, I guess." He glanced at his daughter, and forced a smile. "And being with Robyn in here. . . ."

"Perhaps I should have worn a uniform," I faltered.

"No," he said firmly. "The dress is just fine. Makes you look . . . very attractive, huh Molly?"

"Downstairs we all think Miss Montrose is attractive, Mr. David," Molly said, smiling. She busied herself setting a place for him at our small table near Robyn's bed.

"Do you mind if I smoke?"

"Not at all."

He lit a cigarette and came to sit on the edge of Robyn's bed. "Suzie and Cindy have come to dinner too I see, Princess," he smiled, setting up one of the dolls that had fallen sideways when he sat down.

"And Diane," Robyn said quickly, smiling at him.

"Diane?"

"That's Miss Montrose's name," she confided.

He looked at me, and I felt color come into my face abruptly. "It's a very beautiful name," he said quietly. "But you don't call Miss Montrose that, darling, do you?"

She laughed. "Oh no! I call her Miss Montrose, and she's nice. She has dinner with me, and reads me a story afterwards. Or we play a game. She's awfully nice, Daddy. Everyone likes her. Even Grandma."

He ruffled her fair hair. "What d'you mean, even Grandma?"

"Grandma didn't like her at first, but she does now. She told me so this afternoon. She said. . . ."

"You mustn't repeat what grown-ups say, Princess. You know that."

"But I'm glad. 'Cause now Grandma won't send her away?"

He chuckled, and glanced at me obliquely from beneath his dark brows. "Well, I'm glad of that, aren't you?"

"Yes, I am."

"But you mustn't take up too much of her time."

"Robyn wouldn't do that," I protested quickly. "It was my suggestion. I hope you don't mind?"

"Mind?" The dark eyebrows raised. "I haven't seen Robyn looking as well and happy since. . . ." He broke off. He added quietly: "Not in a long, long time. I'm extremely grateful, Miss Montrose." It was not idly said. His voice held deep feeling. I looked away, embarrassed.

"I like being in here with Robyn," I said.

He nodded, studying me. "I'm glad of that." He glanced at the maid. "Ready, Molly? We can manage if you want to go back downstairs. Will you tell my uncle and the others that I'm dining up here tonight? I'll join them later. But I'll be having coffee with my mother."

"Yes, Mr. David," Molly smiled.

He came and sat down opposite me. He started talking easily, including Robyn and the dolls in his conversation as though it was the most natural thing that we should be together in Robyn's bedroom eating what proved to be an excellent dinner.

The wine was light and dry, and I could feel its warmth entering me. I read Robyn a story on his insistence that we keep to our normal routine. And afterwards I prepared her for her night's rest, while he watched us both silently, a slight frown creasing his forehead above the brown eyes.

I patted Robyn's shoulder, and she caught my hand and squeezed it.

"Good night, Robyn. Goodnight, Mr. Warburton."

He walked to the door with me. "Must you go?"

I nodded. "Robyn must have her sleep. And

I still have Mrs. Warburton to see when you've finished your coffee."

He frowned. "I'd like to talk to you afterwards. May I? I feel that I owe you an explanation. I. . . ." He hesitated and glanced at Robyn where she watched him with the covers drawn up to her chin, and the two dolls now in bed with her, one on either side.

I smiled. "It really isn't necessary, Mr. Warburton. Bob Jensen told me all about your wife's . . . about the accident and all. Perhaps it would be better if you got someone else to. . . ."

"No, no," he interrupted. "I would like you to stay." He paused and shook his head. "So Bob noticed it, too? Poor Bob." He glanced at Robyn watching us both silently. "And someone else I think, though perhaps not consciously. Well, I'll talk to you about that, if you're too tired tonight. . . ."

"It isn't that I'm too tired," I said quickly. "If it concerns Robyn. . . ?"

He nodded. "It does. I'll be in the library when you're finished up here. If it's not too much trouble to come down?"

"It's no trouble."

"Then I won't say goodnight." He turned abruptly to Robyn, and I walked towards the door. He seemed to have forgotten me as I looked back. He had bent over Robyn, and she was clinging to him with both her thin little arms wrapped around his neck.

I closed the door gently, and went to my room. I changed into a white uniform quickly, and went to Martha Warburton.

She looked up suspiciously as I came in. "Where did you have your dinner tonight, Montrose?" she demanded.

"With Robyn, Mrs. Warburton."

"David usually has dinner with her when he's at Ravensnest."

"Yes, he came in. Molly brought his dinner up."

She scowled at me. "So you had dinner together in there with Robyn? What d'you think of my son, Montrose?"

I smiled because she had said that as though she only possessed one son. "Which son, Mrs. Warburton?"

"You know who I mean. David."

I said carefully: "If it's possible to form an opinion about anyone so quickly—I'd say he was the kind of son any woman could be proud of."

"I'm asking you what you as a young woman thought of my son as a man? You're not a mother yet, are you?"

I colored, and fought indignation briefly. But the ground I had won with Martha Warburton I did not want to lose now.

"He's very good-looking, of course," I said

nervously. "He seemed friendly and gentle, and anyone can see that he's devoted to Robyn. But he's not a happy man, Mrs. Warburton. I would say his wife's death has saddened him. He misses her badly. He must have loved her very deeply."

She nodded, studying me. "You're an observant young woman, Montrose. Don't miss much, do you? Do you find David attractive?"

"Most women would."

She sniffed. "You look a normal, healthy young woman to me, Montrose. And you're pretty. David could do worse. . . ." She said it grudgingly.

I laughed. "Really, Mrs. Warburton. Are you trying to play Cupid?" That would be absolutely too much—I found the thought amusing as I looked at her.

She made an angry sound, and lapsed into sulky silence. She sighed when I had finished, and made her comfortable.

"You're a good nurse, Montrose," she admitted. "You're doing more for me than that old fool Chester has done in years. Why didn't *he* do these things?"

"Possibly because they're nursing procedures, and he's a busy G. P., Mrs. Warburton. Mrs. Rathbone couldn't do them correctly unless she was trained. You need a nurse, and you are going to need one for some time. If I leave Ravensnest, you should find another. But make sure she's an R.N. and trained in physiotherapy. Exercise is the only way to restore the muscles. If you don't have it, it would mean a choice between painful rehabilitation after prolonged surgery, or a wheelchair."

"Nobody is going to put *me* in a wheelchair," she said indignantly.

"Then keep up the passive exercises I've shown you. Use the arm and leg movements every chance. Promise?"

Except for when she looked at Robyn, it was the first time I had seen her smile. "Goodnight, Mrs. Warburton."

"Montrose!"

I stopped with my hand on the door. "Yes?"

"I'll try. Never yet gave in easily. Thank you, Montrose."

The light was out in Robyn's room, the door closed. I sighed in relief that the chores were over and went downstairs, aware of an unaccountable elation that I tried to subdue, but suspected sprang from anticipation of talking to David Warburton again.

Kerr Warburton and Isabel looked up from where they sat sipping drinks in the big lounge. Neither Clive nor Kerr's wife were in sight, but Kerr waved lazily, and grinned at me as though yesterday's unpleasant incident had never happened.

"Come and relax with us, Miss Montrose,

over a scotch. Do you good. You shouldn't work all the time, you know."

"Yes. Please join us, Miss Montrose," Isabel called. Her face was flushed, and she looked a little high. I frowned. They had been sitting close together on the divan, and their movement as they saw me and separated had seemed hurried, guilty. I remembered that they were cousins, but I remembered also that Martha had married her cousin. Inbreeding did not appear to bother the Warburtons.

"Sorry! I'm not through yet," I called back. "Perhaps later."

I knocked and went into the library, aware of their suddenly intense interest that signified they knew David was there.

He looked up from where he sat at the huge table as I came in, an old book with parchment pages open before him, his thick black hair a little disturbed as though he'd been running his fingers through it as he read.

"Hello. You made it," he said cheerfully.

"Your mother has had her physiotherapy, and Robyn seems sleeping. Which marks the end of my day, unless either of them needs me through the night."

"My mother won't disturb you. She's too independent. Robyn told me you'd said she must call you if she needed anything or was frightened in the night."

"Bryant has put in a bell for us. She has only to press the button and it rings in my room."

He smiled. "Like in a hospital?"

"Yes."

"Wouldn't that be rather a temptation for a little girl? To ring in every now and then to see if you come?"

I smiled. "Perhaps. All the same, if she wakes in the night there has to be a reason."

He nodded, studying me. "Yes, I suppose there would." He gestured to a chair near his. "Won't you sit down? Can I get you a drink? A highball?"

I shook my head, and sat down, aware of embarrassment because the admiration in his eyes was so frank and disarming.

"Don't you drink, Miss Montrose?" he asked, surprised.

"On occasions, yes. But never on duty, naturally."

"You're not on duty now," he said, frowning.

I shrugged. "You sent for me. What was it you wanted, Mr. Warburton?"

"I just wanted to explain to you about Robyn. But that doesn't mean you're still on duty." He smiled. "Let me get you a drink? Please?"

"Well. . . ."

He sprang up and walked to a small cabinet. Ice tinkled as he worked. He came back with two tall glasses, the drinks long and cool and refreshing.

"You've heard how my wife . . . how Robyn's mother died?" He leaned back in his chair, watching me.

"Yes. Mr. Prince mentioned it and Bob Jensen told me more. It must have been . . . very tragic for you both." I sipped, starting to relax; the drink was just right. But I would have to make some kind of rule for myself about such things as drinks in the library tête-à-tête with David Warburton. In hospitals such things were simple enough. You worked set hours. You were either on duty, or off duty. There was nothing in between. But in private nursing I was going to have to make my own rules.

"It was tragic for both of us," he said somberly. "But especially so for Robyn. Did Chester tell you that Robyn has no memory of her mother, or her death?"

I frowned. "No, he did not!"

He nodded. "Robyn had an almost complete mental and physical breakdown after we found . . . Linda's body off Wreck Beach. She has always been delicate. Rheumatic fever mostly, as she still has. But this was different, and to me . . . a terrible thing. Chester sent her to a psychiatrist. A child eight years old. . . !"

I nodded, sympathetically. "The emotional shock?"

"Yes. He called it a traumatic psychosis, from emotional shock. She was completely paralyzed for months. But eventually she responded to treatment and recovered normal control of the function of her muscles. It weakened her, though, and of course when she returned home to Ravensnest, the rheumatic fever, the heart complications returned again worse than they'd been before."

"And Robyn had closed her mind against memory of her mother's death, and . . . and what she had seen at Wreck Beach?"

He nodded. "Yes. And I think it's better to leave it that way. Sometimes I think nature has her own way of healing such hurt. I wish that I could forget, as Robyn has. They wanted her to have further treatment, but I would not allow it. Why bring back *that* memory? Why?"

He had forgotten me, I saw, in that moment. I said quietly: "Because in morbid mental conditions, Mr. Warburton, the automatic recall of a memory like that is often retained, after conscious recall has been lost as it is lost with Robyn. The memory is still there, but hidden, locked away, changed, often replaced by . . . by fantasy."

"You mean Robyn's mind might replace what really happened with an imaginary event?" He went on slowly. "Miss Montrose, it has, and does. Sometimes she thinks it is something that happened to her, or to me, or to her grandmother. She wakes crying. Sometimes she cries out like an epileptic. Perhaps what she sees is grim and terrifying—but I'm sure of one thing. It can never be as ... as horrible as seeing her mother's body in the water. It can never be as terrible as the reality. Never! Believe me, I know. Oh, I'll tell her one day, when she's old enough to understand. But not yet. She's too young to be tortured again. It's better to forget, to write off what she imagines as dreams since usually they come at night. Don't you agree?"

His eyes appealed to me. I shook my head, and finished the drink. "I'm only a nurse, Mr. Warburton, not a psychiatrist. Nursing taught me that it is better to bring such things out into the open, and face them. It's healthier that way. Hidden, they can grow more terrible than the reality."

He studied me. "If Robyn was your child, what would you do?"

I frowned at him. It did not seem a fair question. I hesitated.

I said slowly: "I'm not sure what I'd do, Mr. Warburton. But I think I'd start by trying to explain that death is change, often release. That death can be kind when it comes quickly and without prolonged illness or pain. Yes, I think I'd start by trying to overcome her fear and horror of death by drowning. I think that once she came to accept that, then what happened could be brought to the surface to be healed by sympathy, and time, and well ... just by living and growing up. ..."

"Could you do that, Miss Montrose? Could you . . . really bring it to the surface, heal it?"

"No," I said quickly. "*I* couldn't! It would have to be someone closer to Robyn than any nurse could be. It would have to be someone she trusts implicitly."

I looked at him steadily. "I think it would have to be you."

He shook his head. "No. Not me. It's still too close. Too horrible. . . ."

I stood up. "Thank you for telling me. If fantasies come to Robyn in the night now, at least I'll know what to expect."

"I thought you should know," he muttered.

"Goodnight, Mr. Warburton."

"Goodnight. . . ."

The two empty glasses and a bottle of scotch stood on the low coffee table near the divan as I left the library, but Kerr Warburton and his cousin Isabel were gone. I smelled coffee in the kitchen, and turned that way as cups clattered and I heard Molly Waters' low voice.

I walked in quietly. Molly was pouring coffee, and Ken Bryant sat at the table, together with another man sitting with his back to me as I came in.

"Do you have any coffee to spare?"

They all looked around quickly, and Molly smiled. "Sure, Miss Montrose. You find my note?"

I stared at her. "What note?"

"Then you didn't? Bob here asked me to see if I could find you. I told him you'd be with Mrs. Warburton Senior in her room. But I left a note under your door saying Bob would wait in the kitchen."

"I hope you don't mind, Miss Montrose?" Bob Jensen had turned towards me where he sat awkwardly on the edge of one of the chairs. "I had to see you tonight."

I smiled because he looked so apologetic, peering at me with faded but still keen blue eyes, his sandy hair spruced and slicked back tonight, his white shirt clean, his trousers creased as though this was some special visit.

"That's fine, Bob," I told him. "I don't mind at all. What was it you wanted?"

"It was about . . . the slicker, miss." He leaned forward, staring at me anxiously. "The one you saw this morning in the water. Ken saw it too, but he says it was just a slicker. He thinks it came from some fishing boat out in the bay. But you, you're a woman now. And often women notice things that men miss—specially when it's clothes. You notice anything special about it? Anything you remember that was . . . well, maybe a bit unusual?"

I frowned, trying to remember. "What did you have in mind, Bob? What should I have looked for?"

"If I told you that, miss, why maybe you'd imagine you saw what I have in mind. Ken said the same thing as you. I didn't tell him either. Suppose you tell me what you saw?"

"Bob, this slicker can't be the one you talked to me about."

He frowned at me warningly. "Miss, that was just between you and me."

"I see." I glanced at Ken, then at Molly. Ken winked at me. Molly smiled. It was not unfriendly. They seemed to be treating Bob Jensen with amusement, but it was kindly enough.

I frowned in concentration, impressed by his seriousness, but not sure why. He seemed so concerned that I had to try to remember.

"It was black, and it had a hood," I ventured.

"So do half the slickers sold in Tregoney or Portland," Ken grinned. "The other half being yellow."

"It was large. It seemed very large. It was surely a man's slicker, not a woman's."

"Women don't go to sea fishing much in these parts," Ken said.

Bob glared at him, and Molly said: "Oh hush, Ken. Let Bob be."

"It was caught by the hem amongst the rocks. It kept filling out when the waves receded. It didn't seem torn, or patched or anything like that. It looked quite a good one. But I can't remember anything special about it."

"What about the buttons?" Bob asked.

"There weren't buttons at all," I said. "I remember that."

"What were they then, miss?" He leaned forward on the edge of his chair. "Tell me that! What were they?"

I frowned. "They looked like the . . . the wooden things they have on Navy duffle coats to fasten them. They looked like . . . well, like wooden pegs someone had cut from beech. And the loops they should have fitted through to fasten the coat were of cord. Yes, I remember that. Fairly thick, strong cord. . . ."

"What color cord, miss?" Bob Jensen asked tensely.

I frowned, and shook my head. "Bob, I can't be sure. But they were dark, not light in color."

"Black to match the coat," Ken said. "They make them that way. I've seen 'em like that, though not in these parts. You sure got good eyes, Miss Montrose!"

"Were they blue?" Bob Jensen asked.

"No . . . I don't think they were blue. And they weren't black either."

"Sort of yellow to match the pegs?"

"No. And the pegs weren't yellow. I told you they were brown, like beech."

"Brown then, like the pegs?"

"No. I think they were red."

"Red!" Bob Jensen was staring at me. His tanned face looked a little sick suddenly. "Are you sure, miss? Red?"

I shook my head. "Bob, I can't be sure. But I

think they were red. A brighter color than the wooden pegs. . . ."

But he did not seem to hear me. "That's it!" he muttered. "After all this time, it's turned up again. . . ."

Ken Bryant stared at him. "Bob, that slicker couldn't have been in the water more than a day or so. Man, what are you getting at?"

Jensen looked at him stupidly, his rather thin lips working as he muttered something to himself.

I said quickly: "Bob, if you think it's the slicker you lost, forget it. I know it isn't."

He looked up at me slowly. "Miss, it has to be the same one. There wasn't but one slicker like that in these parts. I know, because I cut the pegs from a beech tree, and sewed the loops on. Buttons ain't no good to a fisherman. Don't last. You need pegs and rope loops. But how. . . ?"

"Bob," I said urgently. "It can't be. I know who owned the coat. He told me this afternoon. It had mold on it from storing in a cupboard, and he said. . . ."

"Hello, Jensen, I thought I heard your voice in here."

We all turned quickly. Clive Warburton was standing at the open outer door of the kitchen, where he had come from the courtyard. He came and stood looking from one to the other of us.

Jensen smiled and said: "Goodnight to you, Mr. Warburton. I brought over some lobsters, fresh-cooked. And some more we can keep alive till they're wanted. I thought Mr. David might like to take a couple back to town Monday."

"Good man!" Clive Warburton said. "But it wasn't lobsters I wanted to talk to you about. I've decided to take the cruiser out in the morning. You got her off the slips yet?"

"The *Mistral?*" Jensen looked guilty momentarily. "The painting in the cabin isn't finished yet, Mr. Clive. Been so long since anyone wanted to take the *Mistral* out that I didn't rush it any."

"You sure didn't. I noticed that. She's been on the slips for weeks. You'll have her planks warping if you leave her dry much longer. How long is it since you last worked on her?"

"Uh, well . . . last week I had to do some caulking on the dinghies, Mr. Clive. And Mrs. Kerr sent Ken here over to ask for fish, lobster and crab to take down to Portland to her folks. And Mrs. Rathbone wanted fresh fish, and. . . ."

"So it's a week at least since you worked on the *Mistral* at all?"

"Been nobody wanted to take the cruiser out since Mr. David went to live in New York," Bob Jensen said defensively. "How was I to know anyone would want her this weekend?"

Clive Warburton shook his head disgustedly. "Sometimes I wonder what we pay you for,

Jensen. I'll walk back with you. If she's fit to use I'm taking her out at dawn. We'll get her into the water tonight and try the motors. At least the paint should be dry if you haven't touched a brush for a week."

Jensen stood up, frowning. "You want her in the water at this time of night?"

Clive Warburton's thin lips twisted briefly. "Do you have a better idea? I've told you I want to take her out at dawn. I've heard your father used to take her through Corsair Strait by night. I thought you were a boatman like your father. What's the matter with you, Jensen? You scared to slide her into the water, moor her and test the motors?"

"The sea doesn't scare me any," Bob Jensen growled. He glanced at me. "Only. . . ."

"Then come on, man," Clive Warburton said impatiently. "I've been telling David for years that the *Mistral* would be better moored at Tregoney than Wreck Bay. She might be ready for sea when one of us wanted her then. Are you coming, or not? I don't intend to wait around for you all the goddamn night. I'll get David and we'll put her in the water ourselves. . . ."

"Coming!" Jensen said, his voice full of suppressed anger.

Clive turned abruptly on his heel, and Bob Jensen followed him outside, his brown face flushed, his eyes downcast.

The door closed behind them, and I looked at Ken Bryant. "Nice type," I said.

He nodded. "Wonder old Bob didn't tell him to go jump in the Bay. I would have."

"Bob forgot his cake," Molly said, almost tearfully. She picked it up and looked as though she intended to run after them.

"Leave it," Bryant said. "I'll take it down to him in the morning. *After* his friend the admiral has gone to sea. *If* he does. Never known him to take the *Mistral* out before, have you, Molly?"

"Not unless he was with Mr. David. He'll change his mind by morning. Didn't Bob say there was a storm warning from the Coastguard Station?"

Ken frowned. "Yes, that's right. Gale warning. Wind and heavy seas coming down from Canada. I'll bet Bob clean forgot that, he got so angry. He missed a point there. Well, that settles it, Mr. Clive won't be going out in the *Mistral* tomorrow. He's the worst sailor at Ravensnest, even counting Miss Isabel who can get seasick in Tregoney Harbor. . . ."

My coffee had grown cold, and I had lost my taste for it. I left Molly and Ken talking together in low voices and went upstairs. . . .

CHAPTER

SEVEN

WATER SPOUTING FROM the blowhole outside my window woke me. Tonight it had acquired a fiercer, more sibilant sound. I lay listening to it, not quite sure whether that was what had awakened me, or whether it had been something else, some more alien sound. I became aware of other sounds slowly, the mutter of a rising sea, the steady slashing of rain, the low moaning of wind around the walls of Ravensnest.

I shivered and pulled the bedclothes higher. The bad weather that Ken Bryant had mentioned had arrived, with the rising tide. It seemed, and from its keen bite I could not doubt that it was, from the north, and by the feel of it from the Arctic rather than from southern Canada.

But even with the driving seas, the blowhole tonight was not making the roaring sound it had made the night before. It was a thinner sound, with the rising spout of water thrown high, but by the sound of it barely reaching the height of the protective wall from which I had stared down at the slicker in the water below.

Lying there, watching the billowing curtains, and trying to steel myself to get up and close the windows, I wondered where the slicker was now. I decided that it would probably be buried somewhere beneath masses of uprooted kelp in one of the deep holes, or sucked back into the deep water of Ravensnest Bay. The chances of seeing it again were minute.

The curtains billowed wildly at my window, the rain drove fiercely against the glass and I slid reluctantly out of bed. Shivering in my thin nightgown, I drew the wet curtains aside and closed the windows, getting wet myself in the process. Rain drove against my face coldly, and I could feel it on my arms. Outside the windows, the blowhole hissed, but I could not see the rising column of water forced up from the vent. I could not see the sea below either, though I could hear it roaring as it pounded against the rocks in fierce rhythm.

Muttering to myself I came back and groped

for the light switch. My fingers found it, and flicked it downward. Nothing happened. The power was off. I could have sworn. Lines down someplace, I decided. I stood still near the door angrily, my mind orienting itself to my still uncertain surroundings, while I pondered the easiest way to get a dry nightgown in the dark, and wished I'd brought a flashlight with me to Ravensnest.

I remembered what I decided was the exact drawer in the cupboard across the room where I had put my nightgowns. I started to move towards it, but stopped abruptly. Someone was approaching my door in the darkness outside. Someone moving stealthily, almost silently, but with purpose.

I froze, startled, listening intently as the sound stopped in the passage outside my door. I resisted a wild impulse to call out in challenge. My voice would have been shaky, I knew. My heart was starting to pound, and my trembling was not entirely due to the cold night air and the storm. Somewhere towards Cape Cauldron thunder rumbled sullenly, and outside my windows lightning flickered briefly a long moment afterwards.

But I heard a sound like a heavily drawn breath outside my door, and the footsteps moved away with the same sinister stealth going down the passage. I let go of my held breath in relief. I remembered that I had locked my door last night before I went to bed. I tried the handle, and found it still locked.

I leaned against the door. No doubt someone had been wakened by the storm as I had. David perhaps, gone to close Robyn's windows. I listened. It had to be David. The sound of the footsteps was gone, lost in the depth of the carpet. Now I could hear only the sea, the wind's sighing and the patter of rain.

I smiled at my own foolish fears and started groping for the cupboard's drawers and my nightgown. I started to find all the wrong things first, of course, as I groped in thick darkness. I found a folded robe, petticoats, panties, before I realized I had chosen the wrong drawer. I kept getting colder as I searched, but my fingers recognized familiar frills at last, and as I drew it out I started at a single quick buzz of a bell somewhere in my room. I dropped the nightgown in my fright.

I had forgotten the bell that Ken Bryant had installed for me. But my mind readjusted quickly. That had been Robyn's bell. I groped in the first drawer for the robe I had found, slipped my arms into it and drew it around me. She would ring again. I decided that David must have woke her as he went back to his own room. He would be talking to her now, reassuring her. He would be telling her that she must not wake me in the night without good reason. I listened—waiting.

141

The bell did not ring again. Doubt nagged me insidiously. I do not scare easily, but there had been something about those stealthy footsteps, the silence outside my room as whoever was out there listened, that *had* frightened me. That was still frightening me, though not for myself now. For Robyn.

My eyes were accustoming themselves to the deep darkness slowly; I could see the shape of my big old bed, and the clothes cupboard across the room. I could see the lighter square of window, and when lightning flickered the curtains and furniture sprang into sharper focus.

I unlocked my door and opened it. I stepped out into the passage. I crossed the passage to Robyn's door and lifted my hand to knock gently.

The door was partly open, and within I could hear a faint sound somewhere. A muffled, uncertain sound, the creak of Robyn's bed, deep breathing somewhere.

Anxiety touched me, and I opened the door.

"Robyn," I called. "This is Miss Montrose. Are you all right?"

I heard a startled grunt in the darkness, and Robyn shrieked thinly. I was running towards her when a rush of violent movement started towards me.

"Who's there?" David's voice, thick with

sleep called anxiously from the main bedroom at the other end of the suite.

I screamed. *"David!"*

Something hit me a violent blow on the left shoulder. I was caught and hurled aside as I tried to block that rushing, dark figure coming from Robyn's bedroom. I felt my head jar against the wall, lights flashed behind my eyes and darkness descended on me like a black curtain. Faintly, before it closed down, I heard running footsteps and Robyn's weak, gasping cries. Then there was nothing. . . .

I struggled back to consciousness with someone holding my shoulders, and speaking to me soothingly through tears.

"Robyn!" I gasped. "Robyn?"

"She's all right, Miss Montrose. Robyn's okay." My eyes focused slowly, and I discovered that it was Molly Waters holding my shoulders. I discovered also that I was sobbing hysterically, and that I had been struggling against the pressure of Molly's hands as I tried to get up.

"There," she murmured. "There. It's okay now. Mr. David has called Dr. Chester and the police. . . ."

I became aware that I was lying on a strange bed in a strange room—a great four-poster double bed with fine lace curtains. It was still dark outside the windows, but a kerosene lamp burned on a low table, and a big torch lay beside it, adding to the light in the room.

As I looked about a dark figure came in through the door carrying a brace of candles flickering in an old silver candelabrum. It was Mrs. Rathbone, and she bent to look down at me, holding the candles low to see my face better.

"Is she hurt?" she demanded.

"She has a lump on her head, Mrs. Rathbone," Molly said.

"Go heat some water in the kitchen."

"I don't need hot water," I muttered. "Just aspirin. There's some in the black bag in my room, Molly."

"I'll get it," she said, sympathetically. "Shall I bring the bag back?"

I felt the back of my head gingerly, and winced. "Please. I'll need some antiseptic. . . ." I sat up weakly beneath the bedspread someone had thrown over me, and had to brace myself with my hands to keep from lying down again. "Robyn. . . ?" I muttered sickly.

"You'd better lie where you are, nurse," Mrs. Rathbone said, not unkindly. "Robyn is being looked after. And Dr. Chester is driving out."

"I must see her. . . ."

I dragged my legs off the bed and sat on the edge swaying as the room grew hazy again. I was going to have to take it slowly, I realized. My head was aching badly, and my eyes did not

144

want to focus. I must have had a slight concussion from the fall.

"Help me please," I demanded imperiously.

She shrugged. "You're being foolish. There's nothing you can do that isn't already being done for the child."

But she helped me, and her thin hands were as strong as a man's. Robyn's room was full of people. Kerr and his wife were at her bedside; Clive and Isabel were talking in low voices to Martha Warburton, who sat bolt upright on the edge of a chair, both hands clasped over her walking stick while she stared at the bed with angry eyes.

Other candelabra filled the room with light, and David sat on the edge of Robyn's bed holding her in his arms, while she clung to him sobbing piteously. Their conversation stopped abruptly and they all turned to stare at me as I came in with Mrs. Rathbone.

David said anxiously: "Are you all right now?"

I nodded. "I'd like to look at Robyn. She may need sedation. She must certainly need quiet. . . ."

"You still look dazed," David said. "Kerr, get her a chair. My God! When I saw you lying there, I thought. . . ."

Kerr brought me a chair, and I was glad to sit down. I began to realize as Kerr looked at me that I was still wearing only a filmy nightgown and a robe. I drew the robe tighter instinctively, and took Robyn from David's arms, talking to her soothingly. Her thin little body shook with uncontrollable sobs, and she clung to me speechlessly as she had clung to David. In my arms I could feel her trembling.

She relaxed slowly as I held her. She allowed me to lay her down and examine her. She was gray, and her nostrils pinched in, with the cyanosis more pronounced at her lips and the lobes of her ears. I checked her quickly, while her relatives watched and talked together in low, anxious voices. I could find no marks of violence on her body, or throat; but there was a deep, darkening bruise on her right shoulder and upper arm, as though a strong hand had gripped her there.

"Is she going to be all right?" David asked in a low voice.

"Physically, she hasn't been harmed that I can find. But I heard her struggling, gasping. I thought. . . ."

"Her pillow was on the floor where he dropped it." David looked at me significantly.

I nodded, appalled. Of course, the bruising on her right shoulder as he held her down, the blue suffusion, the pillow over her face. . . . Whoever had rushed past me from this room had tried to suffocate Robyn with her pillow. And he had almost succeeded. In another minute or two he would have succeeded if I had not come in. . . .

"Did you see the prowler, Miss Montrose? Could you identify him?"

I glanced around at Clive Warburton, who was inspecting me with those sharp brown eyes.

"Him? I can only guess that it was a man, Mr. Warburton. It was too dark in here to see. And what happened was too fast." I touched my shoulder, and winced. "Whoever it was hit me, and threw me aside. When I fell I hit my head and passed out."

"Luckily I heard you call me," David said. "I was sleeping deeply, I think. I tried to switch on the lights. There were none. He was gone, if it was a man. I stumbled over you. Robyn was screaming. I picked her up and called for Clive. Kerr came first with a flashlight, and I saw you lying against the wall." He fumbled at the drawer of Robyn's bedside table. "This was lying on the table beside Robyn."

It was the hypodermic I had used for Martha Warburton's injection. It had a needle fitted, and the plunger was drawn back, the cylinder full of air. I stared at it. I was not thinking clearly. But I knew that a hypodermic syringe full of air could be a deadly weapon. It could inject a great bubble of air into a vein, creating an air embolism that must kill instantly if it reached the heart.

147

"I don't think you should touch that," I said. "The police may want to check it."

"Seems an odd thing to try to steal," Kerr's voice said. "Where the hell's Bryant? I sent him to check the fuse box. . . ."

As he said it the lights came on, paling the candles and the flashlights. I saw then that everyone in the room wore their nightclothes. Except Clive Warburton. Clive was wearing a shirt and pants under his robe.

Robyn's hysterical sobbing went on and on, her thin shoulders shook. Molly came in with my bag, hovering near the door until I called her.

"Get me two glasses and a jug of water, Molly. I'll have to give her sedation. I'm afraid it can't wait until Dr. Chester gets here."

"Yes, miss."

I made the child swallow one of the tiny phenobarb tablets. I took some aspirin myself, hoping it would dull the throbbing in my head. I watched the child start to calm slowly under the hypnotic.

I looked at David. "It might be better if everyone left the room, Mr. Warburton, except Mrs. Warburton Senior and yourself."

He nodded and looked at them. "Clive, Kerr, you don't mind?"

"No, of course not," Clive said. "Kerr, I don't know about you, but I need a drink. However did the fellow get in? Has anyone missed anything? We should start checking before the police get here. . . ."

They went out, with the women following. I heard Ken Bryant's voice outside, talking softly, both men asking him questions. He came in hesitantly.

"Mr. David."

"Yes, Ken?"

"It wasn't any blackout. Someone tampered with the lights. The switch was out, and the cover of the box was open the way they'd left it."

"My God!" David muttered. He looked at me apologetically. "We've never had a burglary before at Ravensnest."

I said: "These things happen." I bent over Robyn, smiling at her, starting to speak to her soothingly. "How do you feel now, darling? Everything's all right. Your daddy's here. And your grandma. You must try to sleep, and forget that you had such a fright. In the morning you'll feel better, I'm sure. . . ."

"Yes, Miss Montrose." She caught my hand and held it.

"There was something else, Mr. David," Bryant was saying in a low voice. "When I went to check the fuse box the way Mr. Kerr said, I found the back door open. The door from the kitchen that leads out into the courtyard. It was wide open, and the kitchen wet with the rain driving in. Looked as though it had been open some time."

"Did someone leave it unlocked?"

"No, sir. Bob Jensen came over. He had coffee in the kitchen with Miss Waters and me. Miss Montrose was there for a while. Mr. Clive came in. Mr. Clive said he was going to walk back to Wreck Beach with Bob to look at the *Mistral*. After they'd gone I locked the back door myself and put out the lights down there."

"You're sure you locked it?" David was staring at him, frowning.

"I'm sure I locked it. It was open, though, and the key still in the door where I left it."

"You'd better tell that to the police when they come."

"Yes, sir. I'll wait in the kitchen."

"Thanks, Ken. Will you ask Mrs. Rathbone to make us all some coffee? Dr. Chester will need something when he gets here. It's a wild night outside. So will the police, if they come tonight."

"Yes, Mr. David. I'll tell her."

I glanced at Bryant as he went out, and saw Martha Warburton's withered face clearly for the first time. It occurred to me that I hadn't heard her say a word since I had come into Robyn's bedroom. I discovered the reason now as I looked at her. She was crying silently, the tears coursing down her cheeks to vanish into the old-fashioned high collar of her nightgown.

Her eyes watched her granddaughter miserably.

Great wealth can be a burden as well as a blessing. It occurred to me that that was something Martha Warburton had discovered long ago. Her tears were for Robyn, for what was happening to the child she loved.

And watching her I knew suddenly that Martha Warburton knew, as I knew, that this was no burglary. She knew that this was an attempt on Robyn's life. . . .

EIGHT

THE RAIN, THE wind and the booming sea seemed to have locked us fast in a small world of our own at Ravensnest. I was sleeping fitfully when Molly Waters brought me coffee and toast in the light of a gray and streaming morning. I woke up reluctantly, remembering that Dr. Chester had got through last night, but the police had not. I was grateful for that. I had felt weak and exhausted when Dr. Chester came in soaked to the skin, to tell us that the road from Tregoney was blocked by a landslide, and that he had walked the last mile to Ravensnest.

But by then, the sedation had taken effect and Robyn was sleeping, and I was the one who had needed his attention. But I felt better this morning. The lump on the back of my head had lessened appreciably and my violent headache had retreated to a dull but steady throbbing.

"Dr. Chester just looked at Robyn," Molly told me, as she drew back the curtains from the streaming windows. "He said to tell you she's awake now, and quite calm. She's playing with Mr. David. He isn't going back to town for a few days. There are some men clearing the road, and the police are here. There's a detective from Bangor, asking everyone questions. He wanted me to wake you, but Dr. Chester said you were not to be disturbed till after breakfast. I heard Dr. Chester telling Mrs. Warburton Senior that it was lucky you were here to look after Robyn last night. He said he couldn't have done any more than you did for her. He's coming to see you after breakfast."

I smiled. "I don't think I need a doctor this morning, Molly. My lump is going down, and I think your coffee should clear what's left of my headache."

She came and sat on the end of my bed to study me admiringly. "Heavens! I would've died on the spot last night if I had been you when that man attacked you. Ken said he'd like to catch up with him. Though what he was doing is Robyn's room, or what he hoped to find there nobody seems to know. Clive must have told the detective about Bob Jensen being here last night. They asked Ken about him. Then they asked me. They asked me if I heard Bob quarreling with Mr. Clive. I said it wasn't much of an argument, just that Mr. Clive wanted the *Mistral* taken off the slips, and Bob didn't want to do it in the middle of the night with the storm coming up and all." She lowered her voice. "The police question each of us alone, so nobody knows what anyone else says, unless we confide in one another. But you can bet that Clive said something nasty about poor Bob, because two of the police have gone to Wreck Beach to bring Bob back here."

"Surely they don't suspect Bob Jensen?"

She shrugged. "You never know what they think. Or what Mr. Clive might have said about him. But anyone who thought Bob Jensen would break into Ravensnest to steal would have to be crazy. *Or* harm little Robyn. There isn't an evil thought in Bob Jensen's head."

I nodded as I sipped the strong coffee. I agreed with that. Bob Jensen was contented with his life at Wreck Beach, and he had been devoted to Linda Warburton. So why would he harm Robyn? No, it had been someone else walking stealthily through Ravensnest last night. And someone with a stronger motive than burglary.

Outside my window I heard the familiar hissing roar as the blowhole threw up its spout of water, and I thought briefly of the black slicker that had seemed so important to Bob Jensen last night. I remembered suddenly that I hadn't gotten around to telling him that he was mistaken, and that the slicker was Clive's, blown from his window.

But I knew one thing. I had been right about those pegs of beechwood, and the red cord loops. Maybe Clive had noticed Bob's old slicker, and had copied Bob's idea using beechwood pegs and red cord. Though I found it hard to imagine the immaculate Clive, who appeared to be as lazy as Kerr, going to so much trouble with a slicker that he could replace for a few dollars if the buttons *did* come off.

I got up and showered and dressed when Molly had gone, putting on the nurse's white uniform. Dr. Chester looked up from where he sat beside her bed as I came into Robyn's room.

"Hey, what's this?" he demanded fiercely. "I thought I sent you word to stay in bed until I looked at that head?"

I said: "It's much better this morning, Doctor, thank you. I had coffee just now, and I've lost the headache."

"All the same," he said standing up. "You're going to sit right down till I have a look at you. And that's an order, Miss Montrose. Can't have her cracking up on us, can we, Rob?"

Robyn looked up at me and smiled, and

went back to her dolls at once. She seemed to retreat into some child's world of her own. Looking at her, I was not sure whether that was a good thing or not. She was paler than usual, and the blue tinge of cyanosis was as pronounced as last night.

But I sat down obediently and allowed Dr. Chester to hurt my lump with his awkward, probing fingers. He clucked and shook his head.

"I should shave a patch of that hair away, and put sticking plaster on your scalp," he muttered. "But you wouldn't like that would you?"

"I certainly wouldn't," I said hurriedly. "It's going down nicely, and. . . ."

"Vain, like all young women," he said testily. "Well, we'll leave it as is, rather than have a major rebellion on our hands. I see you've used antiseptic. I don't have to tell *you* how infectious human hair can be. But you watch that. The skin is broken. Show me your shoulder."

"My shoulder is okay. . . ."

"Do as I say."

I winced as I reached to unbutton the uniform. My shoulder was sore. I slipped one arm out of the sleeve, and eased the strap of my slip off my shoulder. There was a round, deeply blue bruise that started just above my left breast. It was sore to his touch, which meant deep bruising.

He shook his head, and helped me readjust

my uniform. "Not much we can do for that. Be sore for forty-eight hours. Try running the shower on it if it bothers you. Hot, then cold. An oldtime remedy, but a good one. So he punched you, eh?"

"I'm not sure what he did. If it was a he. My head hit the wall about then."

"I know the kind of bruise a punch makes, when I see one," he growled. "You have any idea who it was?"

I shook my head.

"The police are going to ask you the same question. Don't hold anything back, Diane. Come into the other room with me."

The use of my first name surprised me as much as his seriousness. I patted Robyn's shoulder and followed him silently.

"David showed me the hypodermic he found. It was mine. The one I left here. Where did you have it last?" he asked when he had closed her door.

"In Mrs. Warburton Senior's room. I put it back into the drug cabinet, sterilized and sealed in the jar you left."

"You know what it could have been used for?"

"Yes, I know." I frowned. "But I don't know why anyone would want to use it, even if they wanted to. . . ." My voice trailed, and I glanced towards Robyn's door.

"Because it would hurt anyone conscious, and they'd cry out?"

"Yes. How could anyone expect to find a vein in the dark, or with a flashlight, for that matter? Under the conditions in here, and with David asleep in the next room it was impossible. Unless of course they used anesthetic."

"Ether would have done it. Soaked on a cloth beneath the pillow. Only if you disturbed whoever it was, if they heard you coming, there might not have been time to use it. And perhaps Robyn woke up?"

"Robyn did wake up. She rang her bell. Just one quick buzz, but the storm had awakened me and I heard it."

"You were awake, eh?" He frowned at me, his pink-cheeked face reflecting worry.

"The storm woke me. I got up to close the windows and my nightdress got soaked. I meant to change it. I switched on the light, and nothing happened. We were blacked out. Then I heard someone outside my door. They came in here. I thought it was David, and that Robyn had heard him and rang for me, so I put on a robe and then waited to see if she rang again. When she didn't, I was undecided what to do. But she *had* tried to ring me, so I had to answer. I came across, and you know the rest."

He nodded, frowning. "Diane, I'm glad you did! What were you doing when he hit you?"

I shrugged. "Trying to get to Robyn. I sup-

158

pose I tried to stop him. I called David, I remember. I'm not sure what happened then."

He patted my shoulder. "You're a brave girl, Diane. Of course, it could have been a burglar. She woke up and he saw her press the bell, or heard it ring, and panicked and put the pillow over her face."

"And the hypodermic?"

He shook his head. "Tell the police exactly what happened. Nothing more, nothing less. I can't believe anyone would mean to kill that child. Can you?"

"People have been known to kill before," I said slowly. "For money."

"You're thinking of Martha, and her will, of course?"

"Yes, I am, Dr. Chester."

He sighed. "I hope you're wrong about that. Now you'd better go down to the library. Detective Keever wants to talk to you. I'll look after Martha this morning. You'll find John Keever sharper than he looks. Got a good brain that guy. I should know. Brought him into the world, and treated him for all his troubles except matrimony since. I'll be with Martha if you need me."

He patted my shoulder again affectionately, and I went downstairs. A uniformed policeman was opening the library door as I left the stairs, and David Warburton came out, frowning. He started to turn towards the kitchen, and noticed me. He stopped abruptly.

"How do you feel this morning?" he asked anxiously.

"I'm fine now, thank you. I understand I'm wanted in the library."

He glanced at the door that had closed again. "Yes. Are you sure you feel up to answering his questions?"

"Yes. And I might as well get it over with."

He nodded, studying me. "You remember what I told you about Robyn last night? Frankly, I'm worried about what this might do to her. Chester seems to think there's no psychological damage, but I'm not so sure. She seems withdrawn. Almost as though she wants to ... well, to lock what happened last night away in her mind as she has her mother's death." He looked at me, showing his anxiety plainly. "Did you notice that?"

I hesitated. "Yes, I'm afraid I did."

"Will you join me in the lounge when you come out? I'd like to talk to you about that. I seem to be loading you with my troubles, but I have to talk to someone about Robyn."

"I don't mind."

"You're sure?" His brown eyes pleaded with me.

I smiled. "Yes, I'm sure, Mr. Warburton."

"Last night up there when you cried out to me, you called me David, Diane."

I colored. "Did I? I'm sorry. . . ."

"Don't be sorry. I wish you'd keep on calling me that."

"But your mother. . . ." I faltered. "The others might not like it. They might . . . misunderstand."

"Who cares?" He frowned uncertainly, and shook his head. "Unless it bothers *you,* it only concerns Robyn and me. That's all. . . ."

"Miss Montrose? Detective Keever is waiting to see you." The policeman was holding the library door open, and beyond him I could see a young man sitting at the table reading something in an open notebook in front of him.

The spell was broken. "Coming," I said.

"I'll wait in the lounge," David's voice said quietly as I turned. "Please, Diane?"

I turned my head and smiled at him. "As soon as I can, David."

The young man looked up as I came in, and nodded. "Diane Montrose?"

"Yes."

"I hope you're feeling better this morning, Miss Montrose. I wanted to talk to you when I got here this morning, but Doc Chester said not till after breakfast."

"I'm quite all right now, thank you," I said.

He nodded. "Sit down please. A rather puzzling business last night, wouldn't you say? Nothing stolen. Nothing disturbed, except a hypodermic syringe. Nothing criminal at first sight, except the breaking and entering, and the attack on Robyn. Don't you find it all very puzzling, Miss Montrose?"

"Very," I said. I sat down carefully and adjusted the skirt of my uniform. "But Robyn was being attacked when I disturbed whoever was in her room."

"When you providentially disturbed him, Miss Montrose. Suppose you had not heard, had not gone in? Suppose the pillow had been held over Robyn's face for another minute? Or two minutes perhaps? Robyn would have died, huh?"

"I would say yes, she would have. But Dr. Chester could tell you that better than. . . ."

"And Robyn's appearance in death might have corresponded with death from the heart condition she has? Congestion . . . cyanosis, I think you people call it. Right?"

"Yes but. . . ."

"Dr. Chester might even have given a certificate to that effect?"

"Wouldn't there have to be an autopsy?" I felt sick suddenly, thinking of Robyn's wasted, pitiful body.

"Perhaps not, if Dr. Chester was satisfied, Miss Montrose. This is not a hospital, you know. Ravensnest is a long way from anywhere." He opened his notebook again, and stared at it, frowning. He looked up. "Suppose he, we presume it was a man, had rendered

162

Robyn unconscious and used the hypodermic? Robyn would have died from an air embolism, wouldn't she?"

"An air embolism is detectable at autopsy."

"And the authorities then look for someone's carelessness, or negligence to blame? Right?"

"Yes, they do."

"And that person is usually the doctor, or occasionally the nurse who had been giving the injections, using the hypodermic? In this case, Miss Montrose, either Dr. Chester or you?"

I felt the color drain from my face suddenly. I said sickly: "Yes, I suppose so. But to understand that, to ... to plan it deliberately, would need more knowledge of medicine than anyone here would have."

"Which of course would throw suspicion even more strongly on one of you."

"But what motive could either Dr. Chester or I have for such a terrible thing?" I asked indignantly.

He chuckled. "None, I'd say, Miss Montrose. Now, look around this room and tell me what you see?"

"Books, naturally," I said. "This is a library...."

"This," he said quietly, "is something more than just a library, Miss Montrose. Take a look at the books on these shelves. Glance at the third shelf on your left, for instance."

I turned my head and scanned the titles

closely for the first time. *Emergency Surgery, General Surgery. Anatomy, Textbook of Medicine, Anesthesiology.* . . .

I said surprised: "They're medical textbooks!"

He nodded. "They sure are. And if a guy had the time to study, he could discover quite a lot about such things as air embolism, rheumatic fever, the physical signs of cardiac collapse, or just about anything else he needed to know, without even leaving Ravensnest. Now suppose you tell me exactly what happened last night in your own way, in your own words. I'll take it from there."

"Well . . . I was asleep, and the storm woke me up, and. . . ."

He shook his head. "I want you to start earlier than that, Miss Montrose." He glanced down at his notebook. "Let's see. Yes, I think we'll start when you walked into the kitchen last night for coffee, when you'd finished your nursing duties. Miss Waters and Bryant were in there with Bob Jensen, remember? Then Clive Warburton came in, and Jensen and he had some kind of argument. . . ."

It did not seem relevant to me, but I started there, and he asked gently probing questions in a lazy way that was not at all what I expected from a trained detective. Most of the time while I talked, he looked down at his notebook, and either made notes, or doodled on the pad beneath the notebook.

He looked up at me slowly when I finished. "You could not identify the man who knocked you down, of course?"

"No. It happened too fast, and it was too dark in there."

"Which could have been lucky for you, but doesn't help us very much, Miss Montrose. He said nothing? Not a word?"

"No. The only sound I heard him make was . . . well, it was a sort of grunt of surprise when I called out to Robyn."

"What sort of a surprised sound? Was it deep? The kind of sound you'd expect a startled man to make when caught doing something criminal? Or was the sound shriller, more like the frightened cry of a woman?"

It was something I hadn't thought about before. I considered. "Now that you've asked that, I believe it *was* a deep sound. The sound a man might make. I wasn't sure before that it was a man. But I am now."

He nodded. "And when you called for help to David Warburton, he answered from the bedroom? He sounded as though waking from deep sleep? Right?"

"Yes."

"Which rules out David."

"You couldn't seriously suspect David?" I asked incredulously.

He grinned. "If he was asleep in the next room, no. Now, there was no detail about your attacker, other than that surprised sound, that you can remember?"

I shook my head, frowning. "No, I'm afraid not, Mr. Keever. . . ."

"Detective Keever, Miss Montrose. There was nothing about the figure you saw that you could associate with any of the men you've met here at Ravensnest? I mean *any* of the men. Bryant, one of the Warburtons, Jensen. . . ?"

"No. All I know about him is that he punched me hard, and that when he threw me out of his way he seemed very strong."

"Desperation makes people strong. Otherwise, I wouldn't expect to find any supermen here. They all get it too easy, except the servants and Bob Jensen. Boatmen have to be fit, and strong. Their job does that to them."

"I wouldn't call Mr. Jensen particularly strong, Detective Keever. I suspect he has heart disease of some kind. He appears to have one of the symptoms at least. And some degree of hypertension. If that had been Mr. Jensen last night, he would probably have passed out. He seems to faint easily. . . ."

"I think you'd better explain that one?"

He listened intently, nodding as I told him about Bob Jensen at Wreck Beach.

"I see. I remember Linda Warburton. I was on duty at the inquest, as a matter of fact. Let's go back to the slicker you saw in the water. How can you be so sure it had brown wooden pegs and red cord loops? Did you say anything to Ken Bryant about that at the time—while you were looking down at it together?"

"No, I didn't. But when I thought back when Bob Jensen asked me, I remembered the wooden pegs, and the cord."

"You could not be mistaken about that? For instance, you're sure there were not just plain black buttons on it?"

"If there had been, I could have seen them. No, it had wooden pegs . . . toggles they're called, aren't they? They were quite large, and so were the rope loops."

"Excuse me, Miss Montrose. Would you wait here for me, please?"

He got up and went to the door. I glimpsed two other uniformed police talking to the policeman on duty outside before he went out and closed the door behind him. Outside their voices murmured together while I waited. The ticking of the big clock over the fireplace grew louder. Five minutes passed, ten, before he came in frowning and stood with the door open, speaking to the men outside.

"Better get those wet clothes dried out. Ask for hot coffee in the kitchen. I'll call in, and contact the Coastguard, then I'll go down there with you. . . ."

He closed the door, and came back to me.

167

"That's all, Miss Montrose, thank you. No more questions for now."

I nodded and stood up. I hesitated. "Has something else happened, Detective Keever?"

He studied me briefly, and frowned. "Yes, Miss Montrose. Something has happened. Bob Jensen has disappeared from Wreck Beach. He's taken his clothes with him apparently. I'm going to call headquarters to have him picked up for questioning."

I stared at him. I shook my head. "But Bob Jensen wouldn't try to hurt Robyn, Detective Keever. I'm sure of that."

He looked at me steadily. "I would have agreed with you about that a few minutes ago, Miss Montrose. I've known Bob for a long time. I know him better than you do. But I don't have any choice about putting out the call to have him picked up. Only the guilty try to run away."

He was picking up the telephone as I walked out the door; I felt dazed. Could it have been Bob Jensen who hit me last night? Bob who had tried to kill little Robyn? I needed reassurance suddenly. I looked for David, but he was not in the big lounge, though glasses and coffee and cups waited on the low table near the divan. The rain streamed down outside. Bob Jensen? That mild, pleasant man? It couldn't be. . . .

"Diane."

I turned quickly to see David coming downstairs with Kerr. David was putting on a black slicker, Kerr carried one over his arm.

"Yes?"

I waited near the foot of the stairs. Kerr grinned at me wolfishly, and glanced spitefully at his brother. "Has it got around to first names so soon? Does she call you David too? My, my!"

"Wait outside," David snapped angrily. "I want to speak to Miss Montrose privately."

Kerr chuckled. "I hear and obey, oh Number One Brother. But not outside. It happens to be raining out there. I'll see you in the kitchen when Keever gets things organized with the Coastguard."

"I don't care where you wait. I just want you out of my hair for a minute." David took my arm and led me towards the divan. "I'm sorry, Diane," he said in a low voice, "but I'll have to postpone our talk about Robyn. Something has happened. I have to go to Wreck Beach at once."

I nodded. "Yes, I heard. Detective Keever told me about Bob Jensen. David, I can't believe it was Bob in Robyn's room last night."

"Neither can I."

"Are you going to Wreck Beach to look for him?"

"Yes, of course. But there's something else. We have a cruiser down there."

"The *Mistral*? What of it?"

"She's slipped her moorings, and gone aground on the beach. It will be high tide in another hour. Keever is asking the Coastguard for help to get her off before she breaks up.

"Clive went down there with Bob Jensen last night to take her off the slips and moor her in the Bay. He had some fool idea of taking Daphne and Isabel for a cruise this morning. He should learn to listen to the weather reports! A craft like the *Mistral* is too good to lose. Of all the goddamn luck! I've never known Bob to moor a boat badly before. He must have been worried last night. Upset. And that makes it look even worse for Bob after what happened. Now the police say he's gone, and taken his clothes with him."

"Did Bob moor the *Mistral* last night? He didn't want to take her off the slips, but . . . Mr. Clive insisted."

"Oh, he moored her all right! I just talked to Clive. He said they had an argument about it. Bob flared up, but they got her off the slips, and Bob moored her. They ran the motors for a few minutes, then Clive came back home. That was before the storm came up last night. Clive thinks Bob fastened the moorings carelessly on purpose. Well, maybe we can get her off before she breaks up if the Coastguard ketch can get a line aboard her."

"Do you believe Bob would moor your boat so that it would drive ashore and break up?"

170

He frowned. "Diane, I don't know what to think. I would have trusted Jensen with my life. He saved Linda's life once. He always seemed to love Robyn. But men change, and Bob has had a lonely life down there for the past few years. It could have affected his mind."

"Or something could have happened to Bob last night? An accident? Mightn't he have gone out to the *Mistral* when the storm came up, to check the moorings?"

"I would have said yes once," he muttered. He turned his head. Keever was coming from the library. He added: "But you forget. His clothes are gone."

"David," I said urgently. "You must look for Bob just the same, in case he's hurt, or. . . ."

He nodded. "Of course. I'm taking Kerr and Bryant with me. We'll search the rocks, and the cliffs around the beach. But Bob was like a fish in the water. He'd never *drown*. I'll see you later. Coming, Keever. . . ."

I watched him go along the passage with Keever towards the kitchen. I turned and walked slowly upstairs. Perhaps from the gallery I could see Wreck Beach and the grounded *Mistral*. . . .

NINE

IN THE AFTERNOON the wind died, and the sky calmed to scattered cloud drifting over high up. The men came back from Wreck Beach grumbling that the attempt to get the *Mistral* back into deep water had failed. She was stuck fast on Wreck Beach, they said, and only the calming of the wind had saved her from breaking up.

David came to me to tell me that they would try again tonight, when there would be a foot more water at the high tide, and the chances were better if the wind stayed light.

"We'll get her off," he said. "I'm sure of it."

I shook my head. Outside the sea boomed on the rocks below Ravensnest as threateningly as ever. The blowhole had grown quiet, but that was because it was low water now.

"You found no sign of Bob Jensen, David?" I asked.

"No. I'm afraid Keever is right, Diane. He's gone. Kerr and I searched his room. Bob has never worried much about clothes since his wife died. His wardrobe is simple, and Kerr and I know most of it. He had a suit that he kept for special occasions, and it's gone. He took some white shirts, and the clothes he wore over here last night when he brought the lobsters to Mrs. Rathbone. He used a billfold Linda gave him from Robyn and herself the Christmas before she . . . died. It was gone, and we could find no money in the boathouse, though he usually carried forty or fifty dollars around in ready cash. He'd taken about what you'd expect a man like him to take if he ran."

"Ran where? It's seven miles to Tregoney, isn't it? And last night the road was blocked."

He shook his head. "That wouldn't stop Jensen. He'd cross the dunes. There's a railroad five miles inland, with whistle-stop platforms. If he'd done something wrong, he wouldn't go to Tregoney. He's too well known there. I'm sorry, Diane. But Keever's right. He came here to steal, but you disturbed him. He panicked. It was Bob who tried to smother Robyn last night."

"Keever isn't sure he's right," I said angrily. "Keever was thinking along different lines, until he found that Bob had disappeared."

He stared at me, surprised. "I'm not sure that I understand what you mean, Diane?"

"I mean that Detective Keever was more interested in someone with access to the library downstairs. Someone who studied medical textbooks. Someone who knew that the shock of partial suffocation to a child with a rheumatic heart could bring on a fatal collapse that could look like death from natural causes. Or someone who knew that an air embolism caused by the injection of air into a vein could cause death that would be blamed on the carelessness of a doctor or a nurse."

"You can't mean that, Diane?"

"No? If there was such a person, David—wouldn't he be capable of finding some way to blame Bob Jensen instead, when things went wrong last night?"

"Does Keever think that?"

"I don't know what Keever thinks," I said irritably. "He seems to be accepting Bob Jensen's disappearance at face value now."

He studied my anger briefly, then smiled. "I wouldn't say that to anyone else, Diane, if I were you. Better let Keever work this out in his own way. Bob can't get far. If he has committed a crime, I don't think Bob could hide that from the police for long. He's always been too frank—too honest. And I owe him enough to make sure that he has a good counsel. There—does that satisfy you?"

I nodded. I was not sure why I had such faith in Bob Jensen's integrity, when I thought about it. It was just an instinctive liking I had for the brown-skinned, friendly fisherman.

"Working down there on trying to float the *Mistral,* I kept thinking about Robyn," he said. "Diane, I'm going to take her to the psychiatrist again. Get the best possible advice. You're right about bringing things like that out into the open. I'll speak to my mother about it tonight. I may take her to New York tomorrow."

"I'm glad," I said. "She'll be safer there with you. . . ."

He laughed. "There you go again. Come up to the gallery with me. I want to show you the *Mistral* on the beach. Martha is up there. . . ."

After Isabel and Daphne Warburton had joined Martha, I stared with the others at the *Mistral* through field glasses. The *Mistral* lay partly on her side close in to the beach. Through the glasses we could see ropes stretching out on either side of her back into deep water where anchors held her back from driving higher up the beach.

With Martha I had felt comfortable. But with the other two present I was not. So I excused myself and went to Robyn's room; David

175

was telling them all that he had made up his mind to take Robyn back to New York with him tomorrow.

Martha looked close to those silent tears I had witnessed once before as he told them his plans, but the other two women seemed unconcerned.

Daphne said: "I'm going to lock the door of my room tonight while Kerr is down at Wreck Beach. I'm not going to sleep until that man's caught! Just think, it could have been you or me he attacked last night, Isabel, instead of Robyn. We're just not safe, any of us, until the police catch him. . . ."

I thought it was a pity it had not been one of them instead of Robyn. I closed the door, and went to her room. She was sleeping. I sat beside her, watching her and thinking uneasily.

I began to think that David was being foolish in telling everyone that he meant to take Robyn back to New York with him. The police were gone now. We were unprotected except for the men. And tonight the men would be at Wreck Beach floating that fool cruiser.

I looked at Robyn. Asleep, she looked like any other little girl of her age, except for the violet shadows beneath her eyes. But she was not. She was a fragile human obstacle keeping a handful of greedy people from great wealth. Suppose the police were wrong about Jensen, as I believed they were?

What David was doing was telling all the other possible suspects that tonight was Robyn's last night at Ravensnest before he took her to the safety of New York. I grew more and more frightened sitting there watching the sleeping child. It was tempting Providence to spread that story. If Robyn's attacker was not Bob Jensen—then it was inviting him to strike again. While David was at Wreck Beach.

Tonight.

Outside Robyn's window the sun shone briefly, but I barely noticed. Molly Waters came in quietly to tell me that dinner would be an hour earlier tonight, so that the men could be ready at Wreck Beach when the tide started to flood. I went outside into the passage with her, as it was time for Martha's late afternoon checks. Before I had finished with Martha, Isabel Warburton came in.

"Miss Montrose, could I see you for a minute? It's Dad. He isn't feeling very well. He thinks he caught a chill this morning down at Wreck Beach."

It took me a long moment to realize that "Dad" was Clive Warburton. I said: "I'll come and look at him when I'm finished here if you like, Miss Warburton."

"I wish you would. He's shivering, and he keeps complaining of headache. I don't think he should go wading around in the cold water tonight, do you?"

"If he's getting a cold or influenza, it would be wiser if he didn't. Does he have a headache?"

"A vile one. He says he's aching all over. But Dad always exaggerates when he's ill."

"Ha!" Martha muttered from beneath her ray lamp. "You can say that indeed. Whatever Clive has is always worse than anyone else can possibly get. Isabel, you'd better go with her. Is he in bed? Show her his room. You'll have a hospital of your own here before you're finished, Miss Montrose. There'll likely be a couple more before tonight's over. The water has a chill in it this time of year."

Isabel followed me inside and sat down. I glanced at my watch. "You've had enough now, Mrs. Warburton. A few muscles exercises and we're through. . . ."

"I've grown to like lying here under this thing," she protested.

"I know that. But you can have too much of it. . . ."

I started her on her exercises. "I'll come with you now, Miss Warburton. I'll have to get my bag from my room. He may need an analgesic. . . ."

Clive's room was one of those that I had thought locked and empty when I explored the passage to the stairs leading down to the courtyard on my first morning at Ravensnest.

Isabel knocked, and his voice said petulantly: "Who is it?"

"Isabel. I've brought Miss Montrose to see you."

He grunted, and I heard his bed squeak as he moved. "Okay. Bring her in."

The first thing I noticed was the stuffy warmth of the room.

He was lying on the bed in trousers, shirt and socks, with the bedcovers carelessly tossed aside. His shirt was open, and I could see sweat beading thickly amongst graying hair on his chest. It beaded heavily on his forehead, and his thick hair was wet with it.

He reached to pull up the sheet over him, and shivered.

"I feel awful," he growled, staring at me. "When the sheet touches me I shiver. I think I'm getting a fever."

"It won't take long to check that," I said. I opened my bag and shook down the mercury in the thermometer. "Open please."

"Damned hocus-pocus!" he growled. "All I need is some aspirin, and Isabel hasn't any. Do you have aspirin?"

I nodded. "Yes, but if you have a temperature it might be better to call Dr. Chester."

"Just give me some aspirin. . . ."

"Keep your mouth closed, please." He grunted crossly but stopped talking.

"I'm afraid you're not going to be able to go to Wreck Beach tonight, Mr. Warburton." I checked the thermometer, frowning.

"Temperature up?"

"No," I said, checking. "But it could go high tonight. I'll give you some aspirin. And you'd better undress then, and get into bed."

"Doctor's orders?" His brown eyes studied me.

"Nurse's orders. Shall I call Dr. Chester?"

"I'll live till morning. No temperature, you say?" He stared at me. "How about the beach tonight?"

"Even though you have no fever right now, that could come later. You would be foolish to go to the beach tonight. Is your head aching?"

"Splitting," he said. "I feel as though someone has been beating me with a shillelagh. All over."

"The aspirin should make you more comfortable."

I gave them to him, and he thanked me.

"Isabel, you'd better tell David Miss Montrose says I should stay in bed tonight. Seems I've got flu. Oh, and tell Mrs. Rathbone to send me up something on a tray, I can't come down. Right?"

"Yes, Dad."

I walked out with her, and she smiled at me. "I think he wants to get out of going to Wreck Beach tonight, and he's glad to be ill. He's like that. You must excuse his room. It always looks as though a hurricane has passed through. He won't let the maid touch it. Or Mrs. Rathbone. I have to do it, and he never leaves me in there alone. When it's room-cleaning time he sits in there giving the orders, and the rest of the time he keeps the key in his pocket. He's a little strange about things like that."

It was the longest conversation I'd had with Isabel Warburton. I left her at my room, and put my bag away. I washed my hands, glanced at Robyn and went downstairs. Isabel was talking to David near the library door as I came down. David glanced up at me, and smiled.

"The police at Tregoney just called Martha. They've picked up Jensen."

"Oh?" I said startled. "Where?"

"They didn't say. Just that he'd been found. I suppose they're holding him at Tregoney for questioning. I'll go down there in the morning. Too much to do here tonight. Isabel, you'd better tell your father."

"Well, that's a relief," Isabel said feelingly. "Have you told Kerr and Daphne yet? Daphne will be as relieved as I am."

David frowned. His eyes told me that he wanted to talk to me alone. "I'll tell Kerr about it now," he said. "We've both been worried about leaving you women alone here tonight. But that's solved now, with Jensen caught, and Clive down with a cold. Nothing for us to worry about." He smiled at me. "Don't go away," he whispered as he passed me. He followed Isabel upstairs.

I walked over and sat on the divan waiting. Outside it was rapidly growing darker. The clouds seemed thickening again, but as yet there was little wind. I looked up in surprise as I heard Molly in the family dining room setting the table before I remembered that dinner was to be early tonight so that the men could get away. Mrs. Rathbone came from the kitchen, switching on the lights. She glanced at me coldly without speaking, and went on her way upstairs.

I looked up quickly at footsteps on the stairs, but it was Kerr grinning at me as he came down—not David.

"Hello there," he said cheerfully. "Like a cocktail before dinner? Manhattan? Martini? No? Then how about a Warburton Special? Recipe of my own, gin, vermouth, dash of bourbon, lime, sprig of mint, ice, and guaranteed to get results. Women love it!"

"No thanks," I said.

He shook his head sadly. "I'm afraid our Miss Montrose just doesn't like me. Maybe I should get a cold like old Clive, or reform and become the perfect gentleman like the noble David?" He lit a cigarette and studied me. "Do you suppose that would make any difference?"

"I'm afraid it wouldn't."

He sighed. "The trouble with me is I'm too open. Maybe I should be more like Old Clive. Or David." Momentarily his brown eyes became malicious. "Bet you thought I was the only Casanova in the Warburton family? What do you think David does with his spare time in New York? Even when Linda was alive, we rarely saw him at Ravensnest. Linda was a lonely woman. And as for Clive, I'd advise you not to sit too long at that frowsy bedside of his, or you might find yourself on the wrong side of the covers, like Linda. . . ."

"I don't want to hear any more of your family history, thank you." I got up and started for the stairs.

"You asked for it by being too prim," he said. "No wonder you're a nurse. Not enough red blood in you to be a woman, I'd say. . . ."

I went upstairs seething. I was glad to close the door of my room behind me. Kerr Warburton was a liar, among other things. Hadn't Bob Jensen mentioned him pursuing Linda Warburton? And that would certainly be in character. That morose Clive Warburton as a lover was not.

Molly Waters knocked on my door to tell me that my dinner was in Robyn's room.

"Such a fuss about poor Bob Jensen," she said. "And the *Mistral*. They were all talking about it at dinner. Isabel and Daphne are going down to Wreck Beach to watch them float off the *Mistral*. The Coastguard ketch is out in the bay already. They've all gone rushing off, but Mr. David left you a message."

I joined her in the passage and we walked into Robyn's room together. "A message, Molly?"

"Yes Miss Montrose. He told me not to mention it to anyone else, but he'd like you to stay with Robyn till he gets back from Wreck Beach." She lowered her voice conspiratorially. "He said to lock the door of the suite, and keep it locked till he gets back."

I nodded. I would certainly do that. It sounded like the first sensible suggestion I'd heard tonight.

"It's sort of scary now that they've gone," Molly said. "Isn't it? With only Mrs. Rathbone, and Mrs. Warburton here, and us I mean. After what happened last night, even though they all seem to think it was Bob Jensen. Me, I can't believe that even now. Can you?"

"I don't know what to believe, Molly. But I'll be glad when tonight's over."

"Me, too," she said with feeling. "Soon as I've cleared away, I'm going to bed and lock my door. If they want coffee when they get back tonight, Mrs. Rathbone will have to get it. Should be my night off anyway. Ken and I were going to see a film in Tregoney, but now he has to go to Wreck Beach with the men."

I read Robyn a story after Molly had taken away the dishes. I gave her a tablet, and she started to doze. I went out into the other room, and switched off her bedroom light. I checked the locked outer door and walked about the suite uneasily. A vague sense of fear within me was growing steadily stronger. But there was no other way into the suite save through that outer door. The windows were high, and I locked them all carefully, including those of David's room.

I told myself firmly that the sleeping child was safe in here with me tonight with the outer door locked. Wreck Beach was not far away. And I remembered suddenly that Clive Warburton was in bed in his room. He might be a morose character, but he would come if I called. . . .

I started suddenly. Someone was walking down at the end of the passage near the stairs, and it was neither Molly nor Mrs. Rathbone. The clatter of dishes in the kitchen had stopped, and the light down there was out now, I could see the windows of the kitchen on the west side from where I stood. I went back to the outer door to listen tensely. And listening I heard a familiar, slow tapping sound. A door down the passage opened, and closed again. I relaxed slowly, frowning. That had been the sound of Martha's walking stick coming from the stairs to her room.

I stared at the closed door, worrying. Martha had hardly left her room in the last few days, and that was on Dr. Chester's orders. She needed rest, not stair-climbing. If she wanted something downstairs, she should have called Rathbone or Molly on her phone that was connected to the servants' quarters downstairs. I vacillated, glancing at Robyn.

I opened the outer door and locked it carefully behind me. With the key in my pocket I hurried down the passage to Martha's closed door, knocked and opened it.

She was sitting on the edge of the bed, with her stick beside her, and she was pouring herself a drink on the bedside table. She had put on a robe over her nightgown, and she was intent on pouring clear green liquid from the bottle into a peculiar stemmed glass that seemed to have a second, smaller glass rising partly from the stem of the first.

She started guiltily and looked up at me, and some of the liquid spilled into the outer glass that I saw now was full of what looked like water. Vapor rose from it as the green liquid spilled, like the boiling of a tiny witches' caldron.

"What are you doing here?" she demanded angrily.

I came in and closed the door. I was remembering suddenly the parcel that Mr. Prince had brought her from Tregoney, and that she had him put so carefully in the library safe.

"I heard you coming from the stairs. I thought something might be wrong."

"Nothing's wrong," she said in a milder tone. "You can go back to your room. I don't need you. I'm not a child, Diane."

"What is that you're drinking?"

She glanced at me. The vapor had vanished, the water changed to a lighter-colored green liquid. She lifted the glass and sipped, and looked at me over it.

"Absinthe, if that's any of your business. I like it. Would you care for a glass? It's the best. French. And potent. Not easy to get these days."

I shook my head. "You know you shouldn't drink anything as strong as that."

"I get tired of light dinner wines."

"Mr. Prince brought you that?"

"That's right. He did. Makes me feel good, and I'll sleep better tonight than your tablets can make me sleep." She put the glass down carefully, and looked at me. "Don't be so prim, girl. How would you like to be a cripple, and chained to this room all day long?"

It was the second time I'd been called prim tonight, and I didn't like it. It angered me enough to retort.

187

"It's your arthritis."

She laughed. "That's right. It is. So maybe I'll be sorry tomorrow. But tonight I'll be happier than I've been in weeks. And I'll sleep like the dead. If you won't join me, ask Clive to come down here. I'll guarantee that two of these will make him forget his fever quicker than your aspirin. And don't you dare mention this to David, d'you hear?"

I closed her door angrily behind me, and my anger carried me past Robyn's door before I realized it. I kept on going and turned the corner.

There was a light showing under Clive Warburton's door. I knocked.

"Mr. Warburton. Mrs. Warburton Senior wants you in her room."

There was no answer. No sound of response.

"Mr. Warburton!" I called. I knocked louder, and listened. There was no sound at all within. Neither the breathing of a sleeper, nor movement on the bed. I remembered his heavy sweating again, and frowned anxiously. I tried the door. Locked. I bent enough to check the lock. The locks on the doors of the bedrooms at Ravensnest were old-fashioned and cumbersome, the keys like those on the belt of a medieval jailer, only slightly modified.

I stared. The door was locked, the key still in the lock, on the inside.

"Mr. Warburton!" I shook the door handle, and hammered louder. Nothing.

I realized suddenly that I was afraid, but I bent to the door again, trying to see inside. I could not, but something held me still. There was a faintly insidious smell coming from the room. Something elusive, yet familiar. . . ?

I straightened abruptly, with my heart starting to pound.

Ether.

I shook the door, trying to think coherently through my fear. I ran back along the passage to Martha Warburton's room.

"Mrs. Warburton! I think something has happened to your brother-in-law!"

She stared at me, a fresh glass of the absinthe unsteady in her hand, the bottle already moving down toward the halfway mark. She hadn't stopped at the two drinks she had mentioned. And I could believe her about the potency of absinthe, for I had never seen anyone get high in such a hurry before. Her speech was thick, her eyes had difficulty in focusing.

"Clive? What's . . . matter with Clive, girl?"

"Mrs. Warburton, you must call the police, or send someone to Wreck Beach for David! Clive's door is locked on the inside, and his room smells of anesthetic . . ."

"Nothin' the matter with that . . . man. Got a bottle of his own most likely. I don't blame him

189

either. No, I don't! It's the way this place affects me lately. . . ."

"Mrs. Warburton, you've got to help me!" I said desperately.

"Then get Rathbone. . . ." She broke off uncertainly. "No, not Rathbone. Told her to go to Wreck Beach. Didn't want her poking her long nose in here tonight. Told her to take that scatterbrained Waters girl with her. Saw her watching me when I was going into the library. . . ."

"You sent Mrs. Rathbone and Molly Waters away?" I stared at her in dismay. *"You couldn't."*

"Couldn't I? Still do as I like here, and don't you forget . . . forget it. Now get out of here. Want to lie down, I think. Had one little extra one, and. . . ."

"No!" I said. I took the glass from her and got her on her feet. When I shook her, her head lolled foolishly, but she mustered anger.

"You stop that! Who d'you think you are. . . ?"

"Mrs. Warburton, you've got to stay with Robyn till I get help. Do you understand that? You love Robyn, don't you? You've got to help me protect her tonight. I'm going to lock you in with her, and take the key. You'll be safe in there till I get back with help."

"Nobody dare to . . . touch Robyn. . . . And

that fool Jensen . . . put where he belongs now. He. . . ."

I got her to the door of David's suite. I helped her into Robyn's room and sat her in the deep chair beside the bed.

"Of all times you had to pick this to get high!" I muttered. I doubt that she heard, her head was lolling forward. But she was safe in the chair. She could not fall, and if she gave herself a stiff neck that was too bad.

She snored as I locked the door, and I hoped she wouldn't wake Robyn. I ran downstairs holding the flashlight I'd taken from David's room, for I remembered the cliff path and that one woman had already fallen there.

I hesitated with my hand on the front door. I could not leave the door unlocked. But I might have to get in again, and I had no key. I frowned, with my heart thumping as I tried to think. I remembered suddenly that Bryant was supposed to leave the key in the kitchen door when he locked it. I ran along the passage to the kitchen. It was there in the lock. I took it, and locked the door behind me. Behind me only three or four lights showed in the dark bulk of Ravensnest as I ran across the crisp grass to the gates. Gravel crunched loudly beneath my feet, but I was outside and on the cliff path.

I walked quickly, with my heart thumping, forcing myself to walk rather than run, knowing how far it was to Wreck Beach. A few stars showed through cloud, but it was very dark. I flicked on the flashlight, hurrying along close to the stone protective wall as it circled the small inlet north of the house. The blowhole was silent behind me. The sound of the waves seemed less. The tide had a long way to rise yet, but when I reached the end of the stone wall I though that I should see the lights of the men at Wreck Beach, and there would be reassurance in that.

Here the cliff path ran almost directly from east to west, so that although the waters of the inlet boiled beyond the wall, I was walking away from the sea. I ran the last few yards to where the wall turned, and looked eagerly towards Wreck Beach. My heart sank. I could see the lights of the Coastguard ketch bobbing far out, but the headland above the boathouse hid Wreck Beach and its lights completely.

Not quite completely, I realized suddenly. I could see *one* light showing intermittently. But it was closer than Wreck Beach, no more than a few hundred yards away. It took me a long moment to realize the significance of that swinging, oddly moving spot of light. I switched my own flashlight off abruptly.

I was not the only one on the cliff path. Someone was ahead of me. Someone carrying a flashlight like mine, someone walking towards Wreck Beach from Ravensnest.

I stopped with my heart thumping. Who? Could it be whoever had been using ether in Clive Warburton's room?

I almost turned to run back towards the house. But of course! Hadn't Martha Warburton just told me that she had sent Rathbone and Molly to the beach? It must be the two women.

I hurried after them. I wanted to call to them, but my fear prevented me until I could be certain. I kicked off my shoes and ran silently after that distant, bobbing light. It started to come back to me faster. A rhythmic shadow obscured it intermittently, a shadow that I knew was the legs of whoever carried the flashlight. I got close enough to see the shadow of those legs like elongated scissors. I stopped.

Those legs wore trousers. They were the legs of a man, and he was alone.

And as I stared, horrified, something happened to the light ahead. It seemed to incline downward as though it was descending, entering the earth itself. Lower it inclined, lower! The light became a reflection, like a will-o'-the-wisp vanishing into a marsh. It was gone suddenly and there was nothing.

I stood still with the skin on the back of my neck prickling. I became aware that I was breathing as though I had run a long way, and that right now that was exactly what my fear was urging me to do.

For perhaps three minutes I stood still on the path, staring ahead into abysmal dark. And frozen like that the sound of the sea came back to me slowly. The sea seemed far away on my right. Too far away entirely. Ahead there was nothing but darkness. No sound. No movement. I drew a deep breath. I flicked on the flashlight briefly and swung its light in an arc towards the sound of the sea.

When I flicked it off again as quickly, it seemed darker, if that was possible. And I had not seen the cliff or the sea at all. All that I had seen was sand, and an edge of dark green sward . . .

No. Not sward. The green was not grass, it was the foliage of beech trees that appeared to be at ground level, but were not. In following that dancing light I had seen, I had left the cliff path altogether. I had followed some other path that led away amongst the sand dunes. Into the secret beech forest.

And now I dared not use the flashlight to find my way back, lest the man ahead of me come out again and see it. I suddenly felt very small, and lost and alone. The only lights I could see where the distant windows of Ravensnest, where a crippled and drunken old woman and a sick child slept in one of the upper rooms. And Clive Warburton. . . ?

I started. I had heard sound somewhere. A

194

stealthy movement. I crept off the path. I wanted to be anywhere but *there,* if the man with the flashlight came out again. I hurried, in my fear I felt the ground beneath my feet change, become springy without realizing its significance. I crouched again, listening.

Someone was coming warily along the path where I had just stood. But they were not coming from the secret forest, they were coming from the direction of Ravensnest. I froze, my heart thumping. Crouched as I was I watched vague figures moving. More than one. Two. Three.... They moved soundlessly towards where the light had vanished. They too disappeared.

I got up with my heart thumping. I started to run, and in my fear I ran instinctively towards Wreck Beach and the cliff path, crossing that nearer path at an angle. It was like running on a trampoline. I bounded and fell, I got up to run faster, and in the middle of a stride I felt myself sinking. It was the most terrible feeling I had ever known, like sinking into the earth itself! Sharp branches tore at my clothes and legs. I seemed to hang by the waist for a long moment before I fell through, and the branches that had not proved strong enough to hold me released my weight and whipped back above my head.

I think I cried out, though it was a cry, not a scream. I was lying on a sandy floor then, with one of my arms across the exposed root of a beech, and the bulk of a tree trunk beside me that, though it seemed no more than seven or eight feet tall, was as thick as my waist.

It was as though I lay sprawled on the floor of some vast subterranean cavern, the trunks of dwarfed beeches forming the pillars that supported its low roof.

But between the trunks not more than fifty feet from me, a man had started up in fear from where he had been digging in the sand with a sharpened stake. He had been dragging at something in the shallow hole that he had scooped when I crashed through the roof of branches, sand and dried mud. A flashlight balanced on a beech root near him, giving him light for the work he had been doing.

For a long moment he stood motionless, holding the thing he had been dragging at. Then he threw it aside, and shouted in fear, and all in the one movement it seemed to me he started up and was running madly away from me. Running deeper into the secret forest amongst the trunks of the stunted trees.

As he ran someone else shouted distantly. He was being pursued suddenly, with more than one pursuer if I could judge by the sounds. The chase swept away from me, but the flashlight still balanced precariously on the beech root, its bright light shining downward.

And the thing that he had hurled aside, and now lay across the edge of the hole he had dug as though in stiffened defiance of him, was a human arm. I could see the fingers bent into a claw, the white sleeve of a shirt stained with earth and dried blood. . . .

I was running too then. Running blindly in the opposite direction, I did not know where, but anywhere to get away from what I had seen in this eerie place! I crashed into the trunks of the trees in darkness that was complete. I tripped over a beech root, driving the air from my lungs in the heavy fall. I got up gasping to run again. Branches caught at me, but in the madness of my fear I thought they were hands, and fought them. Earth in great dry clods rained down upon me as I struggled, and sand almost stifled me as it ran down upon my head and shoulders. But in my frantic struggling I seemed fighting my way upward, and presently on the sloping sand the resistance to my wild plunging lessened, and I fought my way clear, to fall breathlessly on loose, dry sand of a dune.

If there had been no exit from the secret forest here, I had made one with the strength born of my fear. There was no longer a roof of foliage thatched with sand and dried mud above my head. I was out in the open, and distantly ahead of me I could see the lighted windows of Ravensnest.

I struggled to my feet and ran that way, sobbing. I ran till my lungs almost burst. I fell, and got up to run again. The gates of Ravensnest loomed ahead. The gravel hurt my feet as I staggered across it towards the courtyard. I groped for the pocket of my uniform and the keys, and sobbed again when I found that the pocket I was groping for, together with most of that side of my uniform was torn away.

I leaned against the kitchen door weakly in despair, but in moving heard the jingle of my keys in the pocket on the other side of my uniform. I cried out in relief. I fumbled with the keys, trying to find the right one, and the lock. I almost fell inside, and locked the door behind me in frantic haste.

But I could not stay here. The man I had seen might follow me, though down there I had known him only as an intense shadow etched against the brightness of the flashlight's light. I was trembling uncontrollably. I could barely stagger towards the stairs, and drag myself up.

Ravensnest looked exactly as I had left it. The same lights were on. The door of Martha's room was still ajar, the door of David's suite still locked when I tried the handle. I breathed deeply in relief. I tried to call to Martha that it was me, but my voice seemed only capable of a shaky whisper. But I had the key, and was fumbling at the lock. I opened the door and went in, and stopped sickly.

The suite was full of the strong, fresh smell of ether. Martha Warburton still sat with her head bent forward in the chair, breathing with a nasal quality that meant either drunken stupor or unconsciousness.

But the bedclothes had been torn from the bed and lay in an untidy heap on the floor near the door of Robyn's bedroom. The disheveled bed was empty; Robyn was gone. . . .

CHAPTER
TEN

MY FINGERS TREMBLED as I used the phone in my room. I had to call three or four times before I was answered by the deep voice of the policeman on duty at Tregoney. I poured out my story in a flood of unsteady words, that he must have found difficult to believe.

"I need help quickly," I stammered. "I must speak to Detective Keever at once!"

"Yes, ma'am," the officer on duty's voice sounded skeptical. "But Detective Keever isn't here. He's stationed at Bangor. And I can't send anyone out to Ravensnest right now. Nobody here but me, and I can't leave the office. Now why don't you just go to bed and lock your door, and. . . ."

"I tell you, there's been a murder and a kidnapping! And I think the murderer is in this house right now. What do I have to do to convince you I'm telling the truth? What else has to happen before the police come here to help us? A second murder? There could be one, if Robyn isn't found quickly. . . ."

"Easy, ma'am," he said. "Easy! Very well. You say your name is Montrose and you work at Ravensnest?"

"Do you have to wait for details like that? We need help!" I cried desperately. "Yes, my name is Montrose. I'm a nurse, and I work at Ravensnest. I've told you what happened, and what I saw. Mrs. Warburton is unconscious. She's been given ether. And the child's gone. She. . . ."

"Okay, ma'am. Okay! Now you do what I say. Go into the bedroom with Mrs. Warburton and lock the door. I'll have someone there in fifteen minutes; we've three men in the Ravensnest area right now, and Detective Keever is one of them. Now you sit tight and do as I said. Don't open your door to anyone, until Keever gets there. I'll call Bangor and have them contact the car out there by radio. Now get off the line, and I'll get Keever to Ravensnest quicker. Okay?"

I muttered: "Okay, officer. Thank you! But for God's sake be quick. . . ."

"Sure, ma'am. Sure. Calm yourself, and lock your door. . . ."

The phone clicked and died. I put it down, and looked around nervously. The passage outside was empty and silent, except for Martha's heavy breathing coming from the open entrance door. I had lifted Martha onto Robyn's bed, and I remembered suddenly that the bed had still been warm when I put her on it. Robyn must have been taken only minutes, or perhaps even seconds before I had entered David's suite. There must be another key and yet I had heard nothing up here as I climbed the stairs or came along the passage. I had seen nothing.

I was not thinking clearly, I knew. I was too exhausted and fearful. If only someone would come. . . . Keever, David, anyone.

I glanced both ways in the passage and ran across into the suite and locked the door behind me. Had the three shadows I had seen creeping past me into the entrance to the secret forest been Keever and his men? But they had been following me, not the man ahead of me. Their stumbling upon him in there when I disturbed and scared him by my precipitate entry must have been an accident. I scowled at the locked door. Yet they had chased him when he ran, and even if they had not caught him they must have checked back to see what he had been doing. They must have seen the flashlight then, and found the body.

My mind raced uneasily, seeking reason in what had happened, but not finding it. *Someone*, I did not know who, had been buried in that shallow grave. Someone who had met death very recently.

I got up and went to the door again and listened. I picked up the bedclothes and covered Martha, still feeling the warmth of Robyn's body amongst them. I checked Martha again, and made her comfortable. If she drifted from unconsciousness into sleep, it might be a good thing, I decided. That might be better than reviving her as I had tried to do at first, and awakening her to the worry I knew right now.

But now I started to worry about the locked door. I started to wonder fearfully if there might not be some other way into this suite. I started moving about, checking. The layout of the suite was simple enough. There was Robyn's room, and the long main room of the suite that took up the length of the two bedrooms and the bathroom in between. I checked the windows of the bedrooms, and noticed for the first time that the windows of Robyn's room were deeply set, the outer wall here far thicker than it seemed to be in David's room.

I thought vaguely of some secret passage in this old house. It occurred to me suddenly that there was a draft of air in Robyn's room, a strong draft of air, persisting even though I had closed and locked the windows earlier. In here the sickly sweet smell of ether had almost gone. Yet it still lingered in both David's room, and the reception room, as strong and fresh as ever.

I looked around in puzzlement. Wardrobes were built into the eastern wall where Robyn's frocks hung, and I noticed for the first time that one of the sliding doors was partially open. I stared at it nervously, realizing for the first time that in my fear I hadn't thought of the possibility of Robyn being in there. . . .

I ran to it quickly, and stopped with my hand on the door in sudden fear. It was from this cupboard that the draft I had felt was coming. I could feel it against my face. I hesitated, then pulled back the door and looked inside anxiously.

I let my frightened breath rush out in relief. I had expected to find Robyn's body in there. But the wardrobe was empty except for her clothes, neatly pressed and hanging in place except for a warm winter coat that had fallen from its hanger and lay on the wooden floor in a heap. I bent automatically to pick it up; and froze, staring. One of Robyn's dolls, the fair-haired doll she called Suzie lay beneath the coat, and Robyn had been sleeping with Suzie when I left her to go to Wreck Beach for help.

And I was noticing something else suddenly. Here beneath the hanging clothes the draft of air was stronger, much stronger. I straightened

204

quickly, thrusting the rows of clothes aside. Some fell, but I did not notice. I stared past the fallen clothes tensely. The light in Robyn's room shone into a dark cavity at the back of the wardrobe. Half of the back panel was a sliding door that had been drawn back and left open. A secret door, leading into a dark and narrow passage. A way in and out of Robyn's room that made it unnecessary to use a key, or the outer door of the suite to reach her.

I peered uncertainly into the secret passage. It seemed very dark and narrow, but the floor was of seasoned wood, dark with age. It had not been used in a long time before tonight, I decided, for the rough bricks that formed its walls were thick with spiders' webs. I could see some that had been torn away from the walls, and trailed brokenly. And I could smell ether faintly in here also, as though it came from some source farther along the passage.

I put my head inside and stared along it. The secret passage commenced here at the wardrobe and followed the line of the outer wall of Ravensnest to turn above the ground floor kitchen to follow at right angles the outer wall that turned towards my own room and looked down upon the courtyard and the sea.

But where it turned, it was lighter, and the faint glow along there at the corner had the yellowish quality of electric light. My heart thudded sickly as I studied that faint glow. Perhaps Robyn was there wherever the light was, in some secret room. And perhaps also she was not alone in there, but with her captor?

I backed out of the wardrobe hurriedly, and turned, searching for a weapon. I had no flashlight. I had lost that when I plunged through the roof of foliage and windswept mud above the secret forest. The only thing that seemed to offer me any reassurance was Martha's walking stick; it lay near the chair where it had fallen as I put her on the bed. I picked it up quickly, and hefted it. It was heavier than I had hoped for. I saw now that it had been carved by hand from some dense black wood that my nervous mind did not try to identify.

But I took it in both hands, and what courage I could muster with it, and forced myself to creep through the wardrobe and into the passage. Trailing feelers of spider's web touched my face and clung there, and once a spider fell into my hair and scuttled across my bare shoulder where I had torn my uniform in the woods. I dropped the stick and beat it off frantically with my heart thumping and my teeth clenched to stop myself from crying out aloud.

Feverishly, I groped for Martha's stick again and found it. I forced myself to go on. I reached the corner and rested, listening. There was utter silence within the thick brick walls of that windowless passage, so presently I ventured to peep around the corner, grasping the stick feverishly.

I saw the source of the light. It came from what looked like a small, square door set in the brick wall on my right, perhaps a foot above the level of the flooring in the passage, and the whole of the opening no more than three or four feet square. The passage continued on past it, following the line of Ravensnest's outer wall.

Right now my interest centered on that open door.

I drew a deep breath and started creeping towards it, grasping Martha's stick so tightly that my knuckles hurt, and I could feel my hands sweating. Against the square of light, I could see the stick shaking as I held it out and crept forward. If whoever had taken Robyn through here was waiting where that light shone, I was sure that he would hear my heart thumping. My knees felt weak, and I had to clench my teeth to stop them rattling.

But I reached that square of light, and pressed myself against the rough texture of bricks, even forgetting the spiders' webs now as I listened anxiously.

There was no sound within that I could detect, but crouching there, listening, I gauged the smell of ether to be stronger, much stronger. It seemed a long time before I could find the courage to peer stealthily in from the secret passage. I found myself looking at another door directly opposite me. I glanced around quickly. This was a bedroom I was looking into! I could see the big bed, the covers tossed untidily aside. I noticed that someone had torn one of the slightly soiled white sheets almost in half, taking one piece and leaving an untidy rectangle with frayed edges.

But the room was empty, and . . . it was Clive Warburton's room.

I stood there, trembling. I ventured to the open door and stared down along the passage towards the stairs that led down into the courtyard, with my mind racing suddenly along new and frightful channels.

Clive Warburton had tried to kill Robyn. Clive had her now somewhere, unconscious from the ether. I must have almost come on him, as he took her from the bed. Perhaps she had still been struggling weakly. She had dropped the doll. And hearing me at the door of David's suite, he could not be sure *who* I was. He had wanted to get her away from there fast before he was seen. He hadn't even had time to close the secret doors behind him.

I shivered suddenly. He would come back to do that. But when he did, he would have disposed of Robyn!

Clive Warburton. It was Clive who spent so much of his time in the library. He would have read those medical textbooks as thoroughly as he had studied Ravensnest's early history. Clive who Kerr Warburton had insinuated was Linda's lover. . . .

And then the whole horrifying truth burst into my mind. Clive had killed Linda by locking her in the secret room, knowing that her body would be thrown out of the blowhole and washed ashore looking as though she had died from drowning. It was Clive whom I startled in the secret forest. Had Bob Jensen told Clive he could identify the slicker as the one he had lent to Linda? Had it been Bob Jensen's body buried under the beeches? But the police had said they had arrested Jensen. . . . Of course. The whole thing had been a trap to force the killer into the open to check that the body was still where he had left it. Only like a fool I had blundered between the police and their suspect. If only I had stayed with Robyn. . . .

Shaking, I clutched Martha's heavy stick. Robyn . . . Clive . . . the secret room. . . .

It was not a torture chamber, he had told me. *It was a place of execution.* That was where he would take Robyn. I forced myself to my feet, and started running blindly down the passage. With Robyn dead, he would have accomplished what he intended. He could go back to his room, and close those doors. And who could prove anything against him then? Who, except me? I could. . . .

At the top of the stairs a man was standing,

so still that I had almost cannoned into him. I screamed and swung out wildly with Martha's walking stick. It was caught and torn ruthlessly from my hands. It clattered against the wall where he had thrown it viciously. I turned to run, but his hands caught me, dragging me backwards and down. I felt his knee grinding into the protesting muscles of my stomach, pinning me down. I saw the fierce, mad hatred in his eyes, and the wet cloth coming, smelling vilely of ether. I fought him, twisting, turning my face away. He caught my hair with his left hand and the wet, sickening cloth clamped down over my mouth and nose.

I had screamed, but the screaming stopped abruptly as I held my breath. And then I could hold it no longer and I gasped and inhaled despite myself, and the cloth pressed harder.

I started to drift. I could still think. I could still feel pain, but I had no strength at all. I could move neither my arms nor my legs, nor any part of my body. I felt his knee release me slowly, and he straightened, muttering to himself thickly, taking the pressure of his hand from the padded, ether-filled piece of sheet. He stilled, listening, the cloth lying loosely over my nose and mouth. I tried to move my head, to shake it off, but I could not. I lay there, utterly helpless. I could hear his muttering as he walked to the corner of the passage near my own room. He stopped there, listening, but that was no help to me at all. He came back and looked down at me. I could sense him there, but could not see him, though my eyes seemed to be open.

He bent over me again, adjusting the cloth, tying it around my face. I felt myself lifted carelessly. His gripping hands hurt me, and I felt pain. Then I was lying across his shoulder with my arms trailing, my head lolling down. I was being carried down the passage, past the corner and down the stairs. He was starting to hurry nervously now. Once he almost slipped and fell with me, and I knew we were going down the steps to the secret room. I heard the swirl of water ahead. His feet splashed into it, and he grunted. It touched my trailing hands coldly. There seemed a lot of water. It gurgled and hissed, flowed and ebbed. It sounded like small waves beating against stone walls. He stepped suddenly into deeper water, for it reached towards my elbows, and it was very cold. It was so cold that it started to revive me. I groaned involuntarily. I think I started to struggle weakly, for I felt myself dragged from his shoulder. My head lolled, and he was lifting me. I felt rough stone behind my head. It scraped my elbows and back, and I groaned again.

The cloth pressed down against my face again. It jerked, and I knew that he was untying it. But there was no relief in that, for the smell of ether strengthened, filling my lungs.

He had taken the bottle from his pocket and was pouring it onto the cloth. I could feel it stinging my skin as it soaked through the cloth and ran down over my throat. It seeped inside my dress and touched my breasts like ice.

And he was talking to me directly, in a low, fierce voice. "I knew you'd come! I watched from the passage as you came from Robyn's room. So it was you in the woods. You! I wish I had more time with you. Interfering little bitch. . . !"

I drifted faster. The ice that touched my breasts moved up towards my mind. Through it I heard his voice only faintly, and half understood.

"Wanted to know about this place, did you? You'll soon know! D'you hear? You'll soon know. . . ."

I imagined I heard him curse as he struggled with the heavy door. Then for a long time there was nothing. . . .

I think it was a frightened sobbing that brought me back; that and the icy cold of water that seemed to rise and fall steadily, for when it ebbed I could not feel it at all, but when it rose it covered my prone body almost entirely.

Awareness came slowly. I felt movement beside me for the first time, and found that my arm was locked around a small, wet figure clinging to me.

"Robyn?" I muttered sickly. "Robyn. . . ?"

She clung to me tighter. "I'm frightened...!" she sobbed. "You wouldn't wake up...! There was something on your face. A rag. It smelled funny, and I was sick...."

I moved involuntarily and almost slipped off where I lay into deep water.

"I'm frightened! I want my daddy...!" Robyn whimpered. I could feel her shivering, as I was starting to shiver now. I felt deathly cold, and deathly sick. My hands reached out to find support as the water surged up again, but my fingers felt only a sloping wall of rock that seemed to lean inwards over me where I lay.

"I want Daddy!" the child sobbed. "I want my daddy!"

Robyn choked as the water reached her mouth, and started to struggle, but I raised her head and held her still. I sat her up carefully, and sat up with her. I remembered that I had noticed this ledge when I had come in here with Bryant. I struggled higher, holding Robyn, until I was standing on it, with Robyn standing beside me. I looked up and could see a single star shining from the top of the vent or chimney of this horrible place.

It was precarious standing there, for we had to bend forward to compensate for the sloping funnel of rock that narrowed into the blowhole.

I squatted with her, talking to her, telling her that her daddy would come soon and take us both back to her room. I showed her the star, and told her that our being here was like a bad dream from which we would both soon waken.

Around us the water moved, rising, ebbing back with the rhythm of heartbeat. Ebbing a little less each time, rising a little higher when it swelled again. The sound of it was all around us, liquid, terrifying. Each time it rose now I could hear the sound of air forced into the vent, though the tide seemed still short of high water.

Panic touched me momentarily, as I remembered the roar of sound the water had made forcing the slicker and massed kelp into the chimney above us. I had no way of knowing how long it would be before that sound was heard again tonight, or if there was anyone up save Clive Warburton to hear it. He would be waiting for that sound. . . .

I forced myself to calm. I remembered that the chimney rose to within a few feet of the level of the paved courtyard, and that the kitchen windows must be almost directly above it. Sound made down here might carry to the kitchen windows, and the windows above if it was loud enough. If there was anyone up there to hear. . . ?

David and the others would all still be at Wreck Beach. But the police could be up there now. I remembered the officer at Tregoney. If

I could shout, or scream loud enough, and with Keever watching the house? Or trying to contact me, following my message?

I held Robyn tighter.

"Robyn, I'm going to try to make your daddy, or someone come down to get us out of here. I'm going to make an awful noise, but you mustn't be frightened, or try to move away from me while I'm doing it. Promise?"

"I . . . promise. . . !" she whimpered.

I kissed her and held her close. I looked up at the star and prayed a little, and drew a deep breath and screamed.

There are few sounds more shrill or penetrating than a woman's screaming. I think it frightened me, and I know it did Robyn. The inverted funnel of the blowhole seemed to concentrate it and throw the sound back at us, shrill and terrifying. Again and again I screamed until I became almost hysterical. I hurt Robyn holding her too tightly, and she shrieked thinly with me.

I remember thinking that if Clive hears, as I thought he must up there, he would find the combined sound horrifying. I screamed without ceasing, feeling the water rising, hearing my voice becoming slowly hoarser, starting to fail. Hearing the rush of air into the vent above us increasing steadily as my screaming decreased.

My voice was gone suddenly. I could scream

no more. I stopped, trembling and exhausted. I could do nothing but hold the whimpering child weakly. The water ebbed, and I waited for it to rise again. Reason came back slowly, and I remembered that the last time it had risen almost to my breasts, and that it had been difficult to keep my balance on the ledge. Perhaps this time. . . ?

I felt the beginning of the new surge, starting to hold my breath instinctively. I felt the water commence to rise again, from where it had steadied near my ankles. It crept up. To my knees, higher. . . . Unaccountably then, it started to recede again. It fell away from my knees. It slid down my calves. It fell below the ledge. I sat still stupidly for a long time before I reached down with my hands feeling for it, doubting my senses. And as I groped in the darkness I heard a sudden swirl of water, a gasp of breath.

Water churned, not far away from us.

"Miss Montrose!" a man's voice gasped. "Miss Montrose, where are you?"

There was a second swirl of water farther away.

"John!" a second voice gasped. "John, are you okay? Have you found her?"

"Miss Montrose. . . ."

"I'm here," I croaked. "Over here with Robyn. Thank God! Oh, thank God. . . ."

I heard them coming. I clung to Robyn,

shaking as they pulled themselves up on the ledges beside us, and Keever took Robyn from me, and the man with him supported me.

"You heard me," I gasped foolishly. "You *heard* me."

Keever patted my arm soothingly. "We heard you all right, Miss Montrose. We tried to let you know we were coming, but you wouldn't stop screaming! Then we had trouble with the door down there. We're going to have to dive through it with you both, and you're going to have to hold your breath while we do it. But we're going to get you out of here, and quickly. You mustn't struggle. You must help us all you can. There's nothing to worry about if you can stay calm. I'm taking you through, and Sam here is taking the child. We're both strong swimmers, and there will be men waiting in the water on the steps once we get you through the doorway."

I will always remember the dive, the groping in the dark water for the doorway, the eager hands that caught us when we reached the stairs.

They brought me almost unconscious to Tregoney, to Beth Swanson's home, and Dr. Chester, for I was hysterical and refused to stay another moment at Ravensnest. I remember the prick of a hypodermic needle, and then nothing, until I was wakened by the sun

217

streaming through my bedroom window the next day.

It was then that David came to see me. He was unwillingly admitted by Mrs. Swanson, who insisted upon remaining in the room with us, her protective instincts aroused. Only I was not sure that I wanted to be protected from David Warburton. He sat awkwardly on the edge of a chair beside my bed, his brown eyes anxious and his face strained and pale. Worry had etched new lines at the corners of his eyes, but he looked as handsome as ever.

We talked restrainedly. He asked me how I felt, and I asked after Robyn. He spoke briefly of the trial that must come. Keever, he said, had wanted to come to see me, but Dr. Chester had forbidden that for another day. Then for a long moment we were silent, until he picked up my hand and pressed his lips to it. He did not seem to care that Mrs. Swanson was watching.

"I don't have the words to thank you for what you did for Robyn, Diane," he said with a catch in his voice. "Or to say how sorry I am that Keever's plan brought you into such danger."

"Then don't, David," I told him. "It wasn't your fault. Or Detective Keever's."

"Robyn has told me how brave you were."

"I was not brave, David. I have never been so frightened in my life." I said.

I shuddered and he held my hand even tighter.

"You . . . won't come back to Ravensnest?" he said at last.

"No." I said.

"Am I. . . ? Do you feel as badly about me as you do about Ravensnest, Diane?"

I thought for a moment. "No, David," I said gently. "I could never hate you. Or blame you for what happened at Ravensnest."

His eyes were tender. "What will you do after the trial, Diane?"

"I haven't thought about that yet. Nurse in a hospital perhaps. *Not* privately again, I'm afraid."

"I can't just let you walk out of our lives, Robyn's and . . . mine. Will you come to see us in New York after the trial? I'm taking her there as soon as possible. It's something I should have done a long time ago. Diane, don't say no. Please."

Suddenly there were tears in my eyes. "I don't have to think about it, David. I want to see Robyn again," I assured him.

"And . . . me?"

"Yes, and you, David."

His face relaxed and he gave a small sigh of relief.

Suddenly we were aware of Mrs. Swanson's presence again.

"I'm sorry, Mr. Warburton, but Dr. Chester

219

said that she was not to be disturbed today. He wants her to rest until he comes to see her after lunch," she insisted firmly, though there was a look of understanding in her eyes.

David released my hand reluctantly and stood up. He followed Mrs. Swanson from the room but at the door he paused to turn and smile at me. . . .

I will always remember the trial of Clive Warburton at which I was one of the Prosecution's principal witnesses, and his sentence and execution for the murder of Bob Jensen.

There would have been a second murder charge if the first had failed, for the evidence at the trial showed that the murder of Bob Jensen had been murder to cover another murder—the jealousy killing of Linda Warburton, whose lover Clive had been in David's absence. Police divers had recovered the slicker with the beechwood toggles and the red rope loops, and there were witnesses to say that Linda Warburton had borrowed it from poor Jensen, and meant to return it on the day she died.

The secret passage between Clive's room and David's suite had been used often enough in those days. It had been used apparently on the night Linda came to him in his room carrying Bob Jensen's coat. On that night he killed her in a jealous rage in the same way he had planned to kill Robyn and me in that horrible underwater chamber. Piece by piece the Prosecution fitted the jigsaw together by skillful cross-examination.

When David returned to Ravensnest, Linda was already dead in the sea. But Clive had told him she had risen early to go to Wreck Beach, and he had taken poor little Robyn there to find her. Under examination, Clive faltered and contradicted himself. As the net strengthened about him, his counsel pleaded insanity. But the Court refused to accept the plea.

It became apparent that some quirk of his perverted mind had made him keep the black slicker. Jensen's suspicion had strengthened when I described it, and he had made the fatal mistake of accusing Clive of Linda Warburton's murder, and had sworn that he could identify the coat as the one he had lent Linda. Clive Warburton had murdered Bob then and there, and buried his body in a shallow grave deep in the secret forest.

After the trial I nursed for a while in New York. I saw David and Robyn often there, and the bond between us strengthened into a bond that I have no wish to break. I have given up nursing now, because David says he does not want his fiancée to work, and besides there is so much to be done before the wedding. And since both Robyn and Martha agree, why what else can I do?

The Warburtons are a very strong-willed family.

But I will never go back to Ravensnest.

To me, Ravensnest has become a mansion of evil.

Other SIGNET Gothics You Will Enjoy